Hunter

7 Brides for 7 Brothers

MELODY
ANNE

Hunter
7 Brides for 7 Brothers: Book Three

Copyright © 2016 Melody Anne

ISBN-13: 978-0692772874
ISBN-10: 0692772871

Cover Art by Edward
Edited by Karen Lawson
Interior Design by Adam

www.melodyanne.com
Email: info@melodyanne.com

 /MelodyAnneAuthor   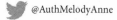 @AuthMelodyAnne

First Edition
Printed in the USA

OTHER BOOKS BY MELODY ANNE

Billionaire Bachelors:
*The Billionaire Wins the Game
*The Billionaire's Dance
*The Billionaire Falls
*The Billionaire's Marriage Proposal
*Blackmailing the Billionaire
*Run Away Heiress
*The Billionaire's Final Stand

The Lost Andersons:
*Unexpected Treasure
*Hidden Treasure
*Holiday Treasure
*Priceless Treasure
*The Ultimate Treasure - **(December 13th, 2016)**

Baby for the Billionaire:
*The Tycoon's Revenge
*The Tycoon's Vacation
*The Tycoon's Proposal
*The Tycoon's Secret
*The Lost Tycoon

Surrender:
*Surrender - Book One
*Submit - Book Two
*Seduced - Book Three
*Scorched - Book Four

Forbidden Series:
*Bound -Book One
*Broken - Book Two
*Betrayed - Book Three
*Burned - Book Four

Prologue

Two Months Ago – Mid September

UNTER BRANNIGAN STEPPED from his rental car, a large black Escalade, and gazed ahead at the family home where he'd grown up with his six siblings. There were memories of good and bad times at the ranch, and the stories that could be told he hoped would stay securely locked in a vault. He'd been restless growing up away from the city and had fought hard to leave. He hadn't wanted to come back. But that had all changed a couple weeks ago when he'd gotten a message from his twin brother, Gabe.

He'd been on assignment in the Middle East, snapping photos as shots rang out overhead. There'd been a message waiting for him on his phone — one he hadn't thought would come for a very long time. His father had died.

Hunter had reread the message at least a dozen times, trying to process it. His father, media mogul Colin Brannigan had recently turned sixty-seven years old. Hunter hadn't even realized the old man was ill. No matter how many times he read the text, he couldn't find meaning behind the short script.

What had happened to his dad? Was it an accident? He certainly couldn't have been ill, or Hunter would have heard something sooner. The only thing Hunter had known for sure was that he wasn't going to find the answers until he went back home. It had been years since he'd been at the ranch, but, oddly enough, after hearing of his father's passing, it was the first place he'd wanted to go.

And now he was there. His dad had been gone for weeks already, and Hunter found himself on shaky ground as he began his walk up the path to the family home his brother Gabe had inherited.

Hunter knew his ripped blue jeans and worn leather coat seemed to suggest he'd shown up looking for a job instead of being a person who belonged there. He didn't care. It wasn't that he couldn't afford new clothes — he could buy whatever he wanted with the money he'd made from his internationally acclaimed photos. He just didn't care what anyone thought of him — family members included.

It had been a while since he'd visited any of them. He talked to Gabe more than the others, but they hadn't been in the same place for … heck, Hunter couldn't remember the last time they'd sat down together. And now he was even more ragged than usual after his long flight, his body still coated in desert dust and sweat, his boots worn and his camera forever scarred.

Standing at six-foot-two inches tall, Hunter easily stopped women in their tracks. His vibrant green eyes had an eternal sparkle to them, and his five o' clock shadow was a permanent fixture. Did he notice his appeal? Of course he did. Hunter was vain enough to appreciate what he'd been blessed with.

He was now thirty-three years old and had been capturing images on his camera for the past fifteen years since he'd decided to skip college. He'd been to war-ravaged cities, places where natural disasters had torn buildings from their foundations, and countries he'd never heard of until he'd set out to capture the best and worst of what the world had to offer.

He and Gabe might be fraternal twins, but they were about as opposite as two brothers could possibly be. Hunter smiled as he thought about Gabe, his incredibly uptight corporate brother, who preferred wearing suits and ties and thought a stain was a national emergency. There was certainly a family resemblance between them, but that's where the similarities stopped.

While Gabe kept his hair short, his appearance neat, Hunter was in constant need of a haircut and shave and his clothes looked like they came out of a Goodwill bin. Hunter liked it that way though. He didn't have strangers always trying to get something from him. They assumed he'd have nothing to offer. That was their loss.

Hunter bounded up the steps and over the large front porch before grabbing the doorknob. It turned without a problem. Seemed his brother wasn't too worried about safety in this neck of the woods.

Opening the door, the smell that greeted him stopped him in his tracks, and his stomach rumbled. That's when he realized he hadn't eaten in the past eighteen hours. He'd managed to grab a bag of chips from the airport on his way out after his twenty-hour flight had ended, but he'd been in a hurry to get home, and he'd munched on those in the rental car.

Now he was starving. He let his nose lead him through the house to the kitchen he'd only been in a few times during his youth, as he'd had no interest in learning how to cook. An older man was cleaning up what looked like the remains of a good dinner and Hunter was hoping there were leftovers. He moved up behind the man without even thinking about startling him.

When the guy realized he wasn't alone, he turned, saw Hunter, then let out an ear-piercing scream that had Hunter stumbling back a few steps as he held up his hands in surrender. He wasn't sure how the windows hadn't shattered, or how a guy could hit that pitch. Even the local bats' sonar had been activated.

Hunter's fingers twitched with the need to capture the look on the man's face on camera. He couldn't pay someone for a shot like that. Hunter heard footsteps rapidly approaching as he turned around, watching as his brother burst through the kitchen doorway, his mouth grim as he did a quick visual for danger. When their eyes met, Hunter gave him a crooked smile and a shrug of his shoulders. Gabe sent him a frustrated stare.

"I see you've come in with a bang as usual, Brother," Gabe said.

"Good to see you too, Gabe," Hunter replied as he moved to the kitchen island and took a seat. They both turned to look at the frightened man whose eyes flashed between the two of them. Gabe gave him a reassuring smile.

"I'm sorry, Mandel, this is just my brother, though you couldn't tell from the homeless appearance he's sporting," Gabe assured the staffer.

"I've been traveling a long way to get here. I wouldn't mind if you passed along some leftovers," Hunter told him with his most disarming smile.

The man was clutching his chest and looking at Hunter as if he'd lost his mind. Hunter wanted to tell him that ship had sailed a very long time ago — that he'd given up on living a life of sanity when he'd begun traveling the world. He thought it might not be the best idea to say it out loud though.

"It's nice to see you've grown up during your travels," Gabe told him.

Hunter smiled at his brother. "And I'm glad to see you've still got a stick nicely wedged up your ass," he responded with a wink.

Gabe's expression never altered as he stood there. He wasn't going to sit down and be on an equal level with his brother — Gabe had to be the boss. It had been that way since they were young. But while Gabe might have a need to keep control, Hunter had managed to talk his brother into some fun adventures anyway.

"You have staff here for just you?" Hunter asked. He still hadn't been passed any food.

"No, I just finished a meal with Josie — the groundskeeper," Gabe told him.

That instantly piqued Hunter's interest. "Josie?" he said with a grin. "She must be one heck of a groundskeeper for you to bring a chef and cleaning crew in."

"I just arrived here today," Gabe told him. "And she was here. I thought it would be good for us to talk."

"Where's she staying?" Hunter asked.

"In one of the guest houses," Gabe said.

"I wonder for how long," Hunter told him with a laugh that had Gabe rolling his eyes.

"I think that's not your business," Gabe told him before looking over Hunter's appearance. "And don't you think you're a bit too old to be wearing ripped jeans?"

Hunter's fingers rubbed against his thighs. "I need the air flow the rips give me. You know I've always run pretty damn hot," he said with a wink.

"Come on, Hunter. It's definitely time to grow up," Gabe said, obviously losing patience with the banter.

"Better be careful, Gabe, you're getting upset which will mess up your pretty appearance," Hunter said with a laugh. "Damn, I think a hair might even be out of place," he added dramatically as he ran his own fingers through his mussed up trusses, which were about an inch past the point of desperately needing a haircut.

He might not want to be as clean-cut as his brother, but he also didn't enjoy long hair. It got in his face and drove him crazy. He wasn't going to admit that at the moment, though.

"Dammit, Hunter. You're here for a serious reason. This isn't the time to be irresponsible or reckless. It's time to have a bit of respect for the passing of our father."

Hunter's smirk was wiped away. "I might not have been the daddy's boy like you've been, but I'm not happy he died," Hunter told him. Oddly, he felt a bit of remorse he hadn't come back to visit more than he had.

"Just because I loved our father didn't make me his puppet," Gabe told Hunter. "That job was reserved for James."

"You and James have always followed the rules, even if it didn't make you very happy. I think you're just upset with me because I dared to do what I love instead of allowing a corrupt world to lock me down."

"Believe me, I love my life," Gabe said.

"Prove it then. Take off the tie, mess up your hair, and let yourself go. I'll take you on the adventure of a lifetime," Hunter said.

He was surprised by how much he wanted his brother to tell him yes. He had to admit, if only to himself, that he envied his twin the slightest bit. There were times Hunter felt the smallest twinge of jealousy that Gabe had roots, friends, a real life. Hunter was a nomad, living for the moment. It was the life he'd chosen for himself, but being back in their childhood home almost made him want to stay.

That was more terrifying than just about anything else he could feel. He enjoyed his life, loved being in a certain country one day and then another the next. Why would he give up that freedom? Certainly not to put on a suit and contribute to the all-American dream.

"I'm happy with my life and I have nothing to prove, Hunter," Gabe told him. "Besides, your adventures always end up with me in a cast." He smiled after saying that and a slew of memories flashed through Hunter's mind of some of the crazy things he'd done with his siblings when they were younger.

When they'd been young, life had been so much simpler. They had always been competitive, but it hadn't ever gotten out of hand. They both had their strengths ... and if Hunter were being completely honest with himself ... their weaknesses. He wasn't going to say that out loud either.

"Okay, well you've gotten me here, so when's the funeral?" Hunter asked. The sooner they got this over with, the more quickly he could get back on the road.

"Dad didn't want a funeral," Gabe told him with a sigh.

"I guess I really didn't need to come back then," Hunter said.

Gabe sighed. Hunter felt guilty. He might be able to harden his heart to a certain extent but he *had* loved his father, even if he hadn't always agreed with the old man, or his brothers, for that matter.

"Dad left us each something. I got the ranch," Gabe said, his voice filled with disgust.

That made Hunter smile. "Ha, that's perfect. You going to sell it off?" It was a question, but Hunter already knew Gabe wouldn't want the ranch. He was a city boy, through and through.

"That's the plan," Gabe said. Hunter didn't know why it bothered him that Gabe was doing exactly what he knew he would. It wasn't as if Hunter would live there even if his father had given it to him.

"You know I don't want to be locked down, so I'm damn glad he didn't leave it to me," Hunter told him.

"Come with me to Dad's old office. Your inheritance is in there."

"What? You get this place and I get something that fits inside the office?" Hunter said with a laugh.

He did rise and follow his brother though; suddenly realizing he'd never been fed. Dang it. He had no idea what the old man had left him, but it didn't really matter. Hunter had plenty of money of his own and he didn't care about possessions. They just held a person down.

He and his brother stepped into the dark-paneled office and Hunter felt a stab of nostalgia as he looked around the room. It hadn't changed one little bit in all the years since he'd last been there. In this spot, more than any other, he felt the pang of his loss. He'd never again sit across from his dad as the old man smoked a fine cigar and they shared a drink.

Gabe moved over to the desk and picked up a small box, holding it out. Hunter's fingers traced over the top of it as he fought emotion he didn't understand. Once he opened it he wouldn't have to wonder anymore what his father's last wishes were. He almost didn't want to find out, didn't want to read his dad's last words.

Gabe said nothing, seeming to know he needed a little bit of time. Because he didn't want to appear to be a sentimental fool, he tore open the box and looked at the items inside. On top, there was a yellowed piece of paper, with a folded note attached, but he was confused as he looked at the words and lines.

Opening it up, he laid it out on the desk.

"What in the hell is this?" he asked Gabe, who was looking at it with confusion as well.

"I have no idea," Gabe told him. They both leaned over as they looked. "It appears to be a ... a map."

"My inheritance is a map?" Hunter asked, looking over at Gabe. Gabe shrugged.

"Read the note," Gabe suggested.

Hunter opened the sealed note. Only a few words were written on it;

You've always sought adventure, so here's your inheritance — a treasure map. You have to follow the clues to find what's been left for you, and more importantly to find yourself.

"It *is* a map," Hunter said. Gabe took the note from him and read over it. Then they gazed at each other.

"Is the note from Dad?" Gabe asked, seeming almost envious.

"I don't know. Did you get one?" Hunter asked as he read over the words again.

"No. No one did that I know of," Gabe said. He looked over the letter.

Hunter found that he wanted it to be from his dad. But there was no clue who it was actually from.

"Why didn't he tell us he was sick?" Hunter asked, letting down his guard.

"He should have. I will be angry with him for a very long time for not letting us be there with him," Gabe admitted.

"Yeah, I'm a bit ticked about it," Hunter said.

The two were silent a moment as they returned their attention to the map laid out on the desk. This was the last thing Hunter would ever get from his father.

"I don't even know what to say about this," Gabe finally said.

"Did the old man lose his mind in the end?" Hunter asked.

"No. I'm told he was completely sane," Gabe assured him.

"I'm not some kid who has time to go on a treasure hunt," Hunter said.

"Then you might never know what he wants to give you," Gabe warned.

"I don't need anything," Hunter said.

"Wait. There's a name and address on the back of the letter," Gabe pointed out as he handed the note back to Hunter.

He read it then looked at his brother. "Who in the hell is Professor Rebekah Kingsley *the third*?" he said. Gabe shrugged. "The third?" Hunter scoffed. "That sounds more like a woman *you* would want to know."

"I'm not a snob, Hunter," Gabe grumbled. Hunter laughed.

"Yeah, says the man wearing a freaking suit and two-thousand dollar shoes on a *ranch*," Hunter pointed out.

"At least I don't dress like a homeless person," Gabe told him.

"I dress comfortably. There's nothing wrong with that."

"Maybe when you're a teenager. But everyone has to grow up eventually."

"I don't believe that. I think we can choose to live our lives any way we want," Hunter countered.

"Are you going to follow the map?" Gabe asked.

Hunter looked at his legacy. One part of him wanted to lift the piece of paper and rip it to shreds. Another part of him — the part that couldn't stand to walk away from a challenge — knew he wasn't going to ignore his father's last wishes.

"Maybe," he said with a sigh as he sank down into a chair.

"You can't ignore this, Hunter," Gabe told him. Finally his brother sat as well. Neither of them looked inside at what else was in the box. Hunter would do that later.

"I have an assignment first," Hunter told him.

"You work for yourself. You can put it off," Gabe pointed out.

Hunter stood. "I have to do the job. I'll be back when it's finished." He turned to walk out of the room.

"Just stay. I'll help you," Gabe offered, shocking Hunter. Emotion he hadn't felt in a long time began to flood through him. Hunter shook his head.

"Maybe I'll take you up on that, Brother," Hunter said. "I might have to find this Rebekah person when I get back and see if she knows anything. I promise I'll come back."

"In another couple of years?" Gabe asked. Hunter felt the sting of those words. He really had abandoned his family. Maybe they cared more than he had realized. He looked at Gabe and the longing to stay there with him scared him enough to ensure he would do the opposite.

"No. I won't be that long," he said, all joking gone from his tone.

Gabe nodded at him and Hunter walked from the room. He had no doubt he would be back. But first he needed to get control over what he was feeling. He walked away from his brother and then through the front door. Leaving was something Hunter knew how to do incredibly well.

Chapter One

Present Day

UNTER PULLED UP the long driveway to Gabe's ranch. It was still odd to think of his childhood home as belonging to his brother now. It had been a couple months since he'd left the place after receiving the box from his father.

His assignment hadn't gone well, as his heart hadn't been in it. He'd been itching to come back home and complete the task his father had left for him. But he'd struggled through the assignment, doing a terrible job, and now finally, he was back where he felt he belonged.

He was irrationally happy his brother had decided to keep the ranch. He was also a bit disappointed he'd heard of his brother's wedding from his brother Luke, and not from Gabe himself.

But he was back home again and ready to begin the journey to find whatever treasure his father had left for him. But today was about Gabe. He spotted his twin standing in front of the house wearing a tux as he spoke with Luke and two women.

Jumping from the car, his camera in hand, Hunter moved over to the group.

"Don't tell me, Frank Muller contacted you," Gabe said.

"Actually, it was Luke. He said you needed a photographer today."

Hunter greeted both brothers and was introduced to Lizzie and her niece while they chatted with their brother Finn on the phone since he hadn't been able to make the wedding. They were interrupted when a helicopter landed on the side lawn, announcing the arrival of James, Aunt Claire and Knox.

Hunter moved away from the group after a little while and took in the area, looking at it through the lens of his camera as he snapped pictures. Maybe he loved photography so much because he was the one in control — the one to forever document the moments he chose.

Hunter wasn't exactly sure. He had no idea what was going to happen in the next few weeks, didn't know which direction his life was going to go. For now, he simply found himself happy to be with his siblings.

Though the ranch belonged to Gabe now, it would always be home — always be the place where he'd created his first adventures, and where he'd fallen in love for the first time.

That thought stunned Hunter; his camera froze and he quit taking pictures. Maybe it was the fact that his brother was getting married, maybe it was being back home, but whatever it was, he was surprised to be thinking about a romance that had happened ten years ago.

Becka.

She'd been young and beautiful and full of dreams. He'd saved her from the ocean and then they hadn't parted company the entire summer. The two of them had traipsed all over the ranch property when they weren't finding secluded places on the beach to make love. They'd laughed and talked of dreams and had left the rest of the world behind.

Hunter had been twenty-three at the time. It had been his first visit home in two years, and he hadn't planned on staying so long. Those plans had changed the moment his lips had met Becka's.

He'd had a hard time letting her go when it had come time for him to leave.

The music began, signaling the start of Gabe and Josie's wedding. Hunter snapped back into the present and resumed clicking his camera, forever capturing this moment in his brother's life.

When the wedding was over, it would be time to find the professor his father wanted him to seek out and get on with his own journey. His brother Gabe had gotten a heck of a lot more than the ranch from their father. He'd gotten a new lease on life. Hunter hoped his father wasn't expecting the same from him. One thing was certain though; he wouldn't know anything until he began the journey.

Chapter Two

SITTING IN HER stuffy office, Rebekah Kingsley III, was daydreaming. It wasn't unusual for her to do that — it would just shock her students if they knew exactly what it was she dreamed of.

On the outside, twenty-eight year old Rebekah had dark hair always pulled tightly into a bun on the back of her head, and deep chocolate eyes hidden by her wire-rimmed glasses, worn more to look like a legitimate professor than out of need. Her normal attire was a pencil skirt or slacks, a loose-fitted blouse and blazer, and sensible shoes since she walked miles a day on the large University of Southern California campus.

Rebekah was a history professor who mostly loved her job. She never had been able to understand those who didn't appreciate the romance and trauma of history. There was so much about it that was fascinating, and no matter how many years she studied it, she would never come close to touching the vastness of the subject.

But Rebekah would always dream. In her mind she would be raiding a tomb in a lost city, her hair billowing over her shoulders, guns tied to her sides, men gazing at her in awe. In her dreams she looked like Lara Croft, not the uptight professor her parents had expected her to be from the first straight-A report card she'd brought home.

With a sigh, Rebekah forced herself to focus as she graded papers. She didn't often get students visiting her during office hours. She knew teaching undergraduate classes was her way to earn her stripes, but someday she'd be teaching the upper-division ones, the classes students wanted to be in, weren't forced to attend by undergrad requirements.

Until she'd been there long enough though, she would teach a subject she loved and she'd do it with a smile. And when she thought she couldn't take another day, her dreams would save her.

A quick tapping on her door made Rebekah jump before she looked up, inwardly scolding herself. A tomb raider would never get nervous over an unexpected sound. Maybe someday she'd go on an epic adventure. She did get nearly three months off in the summer. Most professors got to go to wonderful places. She was stuck in a small apartment in Malibu Canyon, California.

A starting professor made enough money to live, but not travel the world, and though Rebekah's parents weren't even close to being poor, they felt it was a good life lesson for her to learn self-reliance from the beginning. It was why she'd worked her way through college, and why she'd eaten a lot of Top Ramen noodles over those years.

She had constantly reminded herself that there was gold at the end of her rainbow though. And if it were easy for her to get where she wanted to be then she wouldn't appreciate the journey nearly as much.

Expecting a student to be standing in her doorway, Rebekah was taken aback when a man looked in on her, a smile of disbelief on his face, his shoulders so wide he nearly filled out the entire doorway. Sparkling green eyes gazed at her as if she were beneath a microscope, and full lips tilted up the slightest bit.

And her heart stalled.

Standing in the doorway was a man she'd never thought she would see again, a man who had once shattered her heart so badly she still wasn't the same person she'd been back then — a man who had left her long ago. When her heart began beating again, it was at so fast a pace, she wondered if it was visible to him.

"Becka?" The word came out a hushed whisper as he looked at her in wonder. He was analyzing her, searching her eyes as he made the connection. It had been ten years since she'd seen Hunter, and that still wasn't enough time. He'd been her fantasy when she had been a teenager. She hadn't thought she was good enough for him — she'd been right.

He looked back at her and waited. Rebekah opened her mouth to speak and found her voice gone. She was a professor for goodness sake — speaking was how she made her living. She wasn't going to let this man turn her into that sparkly-eyed little girl she'd once been.

Clearing her throat, she nodded. "I'm professor Rebekah Kingsley," she corrected him, deciding to leave off "the third." She actually hated it. When she'd been younger, she'd thought it was sort of cool, but then as she'd aged, kids had looked at her like she was an alien when she said it. Some thought she was a snob, others just thought she was a geek. Either way, she didn't appreciate her parents adding it to her birth certificate.

Hunter stood in the doorway looking at her with disbelief. Rebekah was used to that too. Though she was a respectable twenty-eight year old, she was blessed with fair skin that made her look more like eighteen — the age she'd been when she'd met Hunter. Her mother swore to her she'd appreciate that in another ten years. But when she was teaching eighteen- and nineteen-year-old students, she'd really like to appear at least a few years older than them. Most of her students assumed she was the T.A. It usually took her a while to convince them she wasn't — even with the glasses and severe hairdo she was still mistaken for a student by other faculty members as well. Rebekah had been asked to leave the teachers' lounge several times, forcing her to keep her college ID handy.

And when it came to Hunter he had only known her as Becka. Their summer together, the year she'd graduated high school, had been pure magic and she hadn't wanted to ruin it by being herself. She'd been only Becka that summer — a free spirited, happy young woman on the verge of becoming an adult. He'd been the one to take her there over and over again. Then they had parted ways.

She tried to get her bearings as she gazed at him in her doorway. He shook his head as if he were trying to clear it. She could clearly see his confusion as she felt it herself.

"No," he said, drawing the word out. "It's been a long time, but I swear …" He cut himself off. She could see he was trying to figure out if she was the same girl he'd known all those years before. No, she wasn't. She could easily tell him that. But at the same time, she felt an unusual stirring of anger rise within her.

Rebekah sat upright in her seat. "I assure you I know who I am," she told the man in her stiffest voice. This made those wide lips of his turn up as he sauntered into her small office.

The swagger of his hips as he took three steps forward, positioning himself right in front of her desk, made her mouth water in an unfamiliar way. She shook her head the smallest bit to try to clear it. She'd been in dreamland too long — it was obviously affecting her brain.

His gaze caressed her face and recognition solidified in his eyes. Her heart pounded that much more quickly. She clenched her fingers so tightly together, her short nails dug into her palms. She wasn't ready for this reunion, would *never* be ready for it if truth were to be told.

"This wasn't what I was expecting," Hunter said with the tiniest hint of a drawl she'd never heard from him before. "How are you, Becka?" He leaned closer.

"It's not Becka anymore. I don't like nicknames," she told him as she sat up even straighter in her chair. The sooner this reunion ended, the better off she'd be.

His hand lifted as if he wanted to reach out to her, and she flinched. If he touched her, she was afraid she would end up in a puddle at his feet. She'd come way too far to allow that to happen. His hand slowly dropped as he gave her a once-over. The look in his eyes nearly broke her heart all over again, as he seemed to find her lacking at the end of his perusal.

"Sorry, darling, but I don't like to waste my breath and your name is a mouthful," he said. He have her a wink and a crooked smile, seeming to pull himself together quickly.

"Why are you here, Hunter?" she asked. If he wasn't going to get to the point, then she would lead him there. At least that much she had learned being a professor.

"I was given your name," he said. She waited and he didn't explain further.

"For what and by whom?" she asked.

Suddenly Hunter pulled out the rickety chair in front of her desk, flipped it around, and straddled the thing before plopping down. Rebekah eyed the chair uneasily, wondering if it would hold up under his weight. Hunter had changed since she'd last seen him. He'd always been good looking but the man had aged well, had bulked up from his wide shoulders and rippling arms, to his impressive thighs. She jerked her face back to his eyes quickly and felt a blush infuse her cheeks, though she'd done nothing wrong.

"Whom?" he said with a laugh. "I've always found that word amusing."

She obviously had his full attention. She shifted in her seat, wishing he'd focus anywhere other *than* her. There was an intensity in his eyes that made her incredibly nervous. The sooner the reunion was over, the better.

"I'm very busy, Hunter. Could you speed this up?" she asked.

"It's been a lot of years, Becka. Maybe we should slow it down," he countered.

"You haven't answered my question," she pointed out, ignoring his attempt at a reconnection.

"What was the question?" he asked. There was a twinkle in his eyes that told her he was playing her. She had a feeling he was acting a lot dumber than he actually was. That intrigued Rebekah, though she didn't know why. She'd had one summer with the man, and they'd both been young and carefree. They didn't really know anything about one another.

She raised an eyebrow at him and gave him her sternest professor look — the one known to make new students squirm in their seats. It certainly didn't affect Hunter that way. He leaned in a little closer to her and continued to smile.

"Ah, about who sent me?" he said as if he was having a light bulb moment. "Your formal name — the name I didn't recognize — was on the treasure map from my dead father."

She waited for him to go on, but he said nothing else. Her frustration grew.

"A treasure map?" she asked. Was this a practical joke? It had to be.

"Yep, the map is my inheritance," he told her, completely serious.

"Your father passed away and gave you a map as your inheritance?" she questioned. She had to be sure she'd heard that right.

"I know you're a professor and all but you don't have to repeat every question or this could take a while," he told her. "Not that I mind spending time with you in this cramped office."

Rebekah clenched her teeth together.

"I don't understand why my name would be on this … this map of yours," she said. She felt foolish even saying it. The man was either certifiable or his family was. Either way, them having her name wasn't a good thing, she determined. There was no way his father could have known what had taken place between the two of them so many years ago. But even if he had, there wasn't a reason he would send Hunter back to her. None of this was making the least bit of sense.

"Look, I don't know what the old man was thinking, but I decided he gave me the map, and there might be something worth finding at the end of it. Your name was on there, so here I am. I would have come a whole lot sooner had I realized who you really were," he said as he looked intently at her. He smiled again as he leaned in closer. "Are you going to help me or not?"

She took in a few deep breaths before responding. She had to remind herself that she'd dealt with many difficult students before, and she needed to treat this situation just like that. It wasn't a big deal.

"No, I don't think I will," she said, using the same nonchalant voice he seemed fond of.

"But you haven't even looked at the map," he told her as he patted his chest. She was assuming he was indicating that it was in a pocket within his jacket.

"I don't need to look at the map. I'm a professor, incredibly busy, and I don't have time to play games," she pointed out.

"Isn't the term just about up? It's November. Don't kids still get a break for the holidays?" he asked.

"That's not your concern," she told him.

"I know how to do my homework, Professor, and I looked you up before coming here. Strangely enough there wasn't a picture of you online, but now I get it. You look more like a student than someone who should be teaching the kids."

"If you've come to insult me …" she began then stopped. She wasn't exactly sure how she wanted to end that sentence.

"It wasn't an insult," he told her, holding up his hands. His eyes caressed her face. "Time has been good to you."

His compliment heated her body in a way she absolutely didn't want. She was losing her ability to think — something else that never happened to her. It had been the same way that magical summer she'd spent with him.

"This isn't going to work," she said, her voice husky. He zeroed in on it.

"There was a time you loved adventure," he goaded her.

"Times have changed," she countered.

"I don't think so. We might age, but that doesn't mean we have to grow up." He looked so relaxed sitting there, as if he didn't have a single care in the world. She wondered what he'd been up to for the past ten years. She wondered if he had ever thought of her. She'd certainly thought of him — a lot — not that she was about to admit that. She needed to get him out of her office, and fast, before she lost her sanity.

She realized it might be her smartest move to just go ahead and look at the dang map. That way she could tell him she wasn't able to help him and send him on his way. She had a feeling she wouldn't be able to get rid of him otherwise.

"I have class in one hour. Let me see the map," she said, pushing aside the homework she'd been grading and holding out her hand.

He stared at her for a few moments, making her want to squirm again, but then he reached inside his worn leather jacket and pulled out an envelope, placing it directly in her palm. Rebekah didn't know what to expect when she opened it.

Hunter laid the map in her hand and she carefully opened it, spreading it atop her cluttered desk as she looked at the symbols, the lines, and the key in the bottom right hand corner. This was an elaborate map. The room was silent for several moments as she tried to figure out the clues hidden within, but there were references that didn't look familiar.

"Can you help me?" Hunter asked.

When Rebekah looked up she was startled to notice he was leaning over the desk, his face only inches from her own. She hadn't even heard him rise. Their eyes connected and warmth spread through her entire body.

The expression in his eyes changed to what she could only describe as shock, then he leaned closer. For a brief moment she found herself losing control — pushing closer to him — wanting the touch only he knew how to do with perfection. That's when Rebekah regained some of her senses and slammed herself backward in her chair, the moment instantly lost.

Had he been about to kiss her? Rebekah wasn't exactly sure. That couldn't be the case. They had shared some passionate kisses in the past, but that was a long time ago. In her new world, men like Hunter didn't show up in her office and throw her across her desk.

In Rebekah's fantasies, those sorts of things happened, but she lived in reality ninety percent of the time. This entire scenario had her beginning to wonder if she'd taken a step out of it.

"I can't figure it out," she told him, her voice quiet and breathy. She cleared her throat.

"Neither can I, but maybe together we can," he offered.

Rebekah hated that she was intrigued by the idea of deciphering the map. But now that she was facing it, the thing was like a puzzle that she had to solve. She didn't have time for it with her classes and students, but she wanted to solve the riddle — even if it meant spending time with the man who had broken her heart.

"Can I keep it here and examine it?" she asked.

His eyes narrowed the slightest bit as he studied her. Then he smiled again as he sat back down in his chair, his body relaxed.

"I think this is *definitely* a group project," he told her.

Then the cretin picked the map back up and carefully folded it before putting it in his pocket. She wanted to reach over her desk and yank it away from him. She was far too civilized to do that though.

"I'm staying at my old family home on the ranch. It belongs to my brother Gabe now, but you should remember it well. Meet me there tomorrow. We'll have dinner and go over it," he told her.

"I didn't say I would help you," she said.

"Not with your words you didn't, but I can see you're intrigued. You want to go on this adventure with me," he assured her.

Rebekah was seething at how well this man, now a stranger to her, was managing to read her. But he was right.

"I don't think this is a good idea," she informed him.

He was silent as he studied her again. Then he gave her that devastating smile. "This might be a pretty great idea actually," he said.

She inhaled. He was too close to her again and his scent filtered slowly through her, warming up her blood and infusing her. She hadn't reacted like this to a man since — well, since him. It was unsettling.

"Hunter ..." His name fell away as awareness flowed between them.

"Just come," he said, his words almost a plea. That tinge of hope in his voice was nearly her undoing. She wanted to do what he was asking of her.

She rose to her feet, still undecided. They were in a face-off and it seemed neither of them wanted to give.

"I will …" She paused and took another breath to make her voice stronger. "I will think about it," she finished.

He tossed a piece of paper down on her desk and smiled. She left it there, not wanting to see whatever it was — especially if it would make her want to help him even more.

"Here's a little something to entice you," he told her. "Besides that, I guess I will accept your answer for now. But I'm telling you, this will be fun."

Hunter gave her one more intense look then turned to leave. She wanted to tell him she wasn't going to think about it, that she wasn't going to meet him, but she kept her mouth shut as he left her office.

She sat back down and thrummed her fingers on her desk for several moments before she finally sighed and hung her head. No matter how much she told herself she wasn't going, she had a feeling she was too intrigued not to.

It seemed that Rebekah might be going on a treasure hunt with her former lover.

Chapter Three

*H*UNTER SMILED AS he kicked up the throttle of his dirt bike and flew through the hills. It had been a while since he'd felt this much speed, and with the sun on his face, the sky surprisingly clear, and the moist sea air keeping him from overheating, he laughed.

His father's passing had been a shock and though he'd taken his map and left again for nearly two months, he was back now. He'd thought it would be the last place he'd want to be, but he was finding himself enjoying it. From the time he'd been fifteen, Hunter had known he wouldn't stay home. There had been something bubbling inside him — a need to travel, to seek adventure. When he'd turned eighteen he'd went out on his own and that's where he'd found his passion for taking pictures.

Of course to call them pictures wasn't doing justice to his works of art. He was right in the middle of the biggest storms when the rest of the people were hiding in their basements. He was in the center of the gunfire when war was at its worst. And he loved every moment of it.

He'd only spent one summer back at home — that summer ten years before. The summer he'd met Becka, had fallen for her, and then had left more scared than he'd ever been before. He hadn't wanted anything to hold him down — to keep him in California. And she'd almost managed to do just that. So he'd left and hadn't looked back. He'd continued his adventures, telling himself to do anything else would be an injustice in his pursuit of individualism. It wasn't easy to be distinct with six siblings. Maybe that was why they'd all gone their own ways.

And now, after traveling for the past fifteen years, he was expected to stay home for another extended period of time? Hunter wasn't sure he could do it. But he was going to give it a try for the sake of his father's last wishes — and because he missed his family, even if he wouldn't admit it out loud.

Getting back to the property, he hosed down his bike, then made his way to his brother's house. Walking through the halls like he owned the place was sure to irritate his stick-in-the-mud brother, but that only made him smile more. His boots were dirty and his hair covered in dust. At least he'd managed to let off a bit of steam. And with Gabe's quick marriage, his brother had loosened up a bit — a very little bit. Hunter liked Gabe's wife, Josie. She was a spitfire and totally the opposite of the kind of woman Hunter had thought his brother would marry. And she was absolutely perfect for Gabe.

Thinking of Gabe and Josie automatically made his thoughts turn back to Becka. His meeting with the uptight professor, who didn't even remotely resemble the happy girl he'd known before, hadn't gone at all the way he'd planned, and Hunter was confused as to why he'd had her on his mind since walking from her office.

The girl he'd once known had laughed freely, had run with him on the beaches, had inspired passion in him, and had made him want to stick around. The woman he'd met the day before was nothing like Becka. Yet he could see his former lover deep within her beautiful brown eyes.

The professor, though, wasn't remotely the kind of girl he'd normally date. She was the type he'd have expected to see with Gabe, or even James. So why was his brain filled with erotic images of stripping off her unflattering clothes to find what changes had come to her body in the past ten years? Hunter concluded it had to be because he'd been on assignment for so long over in the Middle East. The sooner he found a one-night-stand, the better off he'd be. Then there wouldn't be naughty images of dowdy professors filling his brain.

"I see you've made yourself at home."

The wry comment came from his left, and Hunter turned to find his brother stepping out of the den as he walked up to him. Gabe looked down at his attire with more disapproval.

"I grew up here, of course I'll make myself at home," Hunter told him.

"My cleaning staff is going to charge me triple with you here," Gabe said. "And it's not the family home anymore."

"You didn't want it," Hunter reminded him. "Maybe I'll buy it from you when you wake up and change your mind about being here."

As soon as the words were out of his mouth, Hunter wondered where in the hell they'd come from. He certainly wasn't interested in purchasing the family ranch. Owning a home was putting down far more roots than he'd ever wanted to put down. Gabe looked at him in surprise and Hunter wasn't exactly sure what to say.

"You know the past few months have changed me, Hunter," Gabe pointed out. He was right. Hunter could see the changes in his brother. There was nothing like a woman entering a man's life and throwing his world into chaos. Gabe continued after an uncomfortable moment. "I didn't know you were looking at property."

"I'm not," Hunter told him as he began to move forward again. He obviously needed a drink since he seemed to be losing his mind.

"Okay," Gabe said, drawing out the word.

"I'm just a bit flustered. I can't figure out the damn map our father left me, and the woman I went and saw seemed just as clueless." Hunter wasn't ready to tell his brother he had once known the professor. He wasn't sure why it mattered. It wasn't as if Gabe would be shocked by Hunter's affair with her so many years before. Maybe it was just that Hunter wanted to keep things to himself.

They reached the den and Hunter headed straight to the liquor cabinet. He pulled out the most expensive label, which happened to be a bottle of Scotch, poured himself a double, and drank it down before turning toward Gabe with a raised brow.

"Sure," Gabe said with sarcasm. "I would love a glass of *my* liquor."

"Oh, don't act so put out. It's not like you can't afford to replace the bottle," Hunter grumbled. "Did I just see an eye roll from you?" Hunter asked with a laugh.

"Quit acting like a little kid, Hunter," Gabe told him.

"Something about being in this house makes me feel at least ten years younger," Hunter told his brother as he poured them each a glass of the delicious Scotch.

"That would still put you at twenty-three. *Hardly* a child," Gabe pointed out.

"Don't you ever just want to let loose, Brother? Don't take everything so seriously," Hunter advised him.

"I'm a responsible adult, Hunter. That's what we do," Gabe told him. It appeared a woman was only able to change his brother so much. Hunter and Gabe had been talking on the phone a lot more over the past couple months, though. That was a positive change.

Hunter moved over to the couch in the center of the room and sat back, lifting his feet and placing his dirty boots on the pristine coffee table. Gabe didn't say anything to him this time. Maybe his brother was loosening up, after-all.

"That's why I like having zero responsibilities. I live on the road, go where the pictures take me, and I have a hell of a lot of memories because of it. Can you say the same?" Hunter challenged.

"I have no regrets about my life," Gabe said.

"Seriously, Brother, loosen the hell up," Hunter practically yelled.

"Or you could settle down and learn responsibility," Gabe replied.

"Maybe we can meet in the middle somewhere," Hunter said. He hadn't come home to fight with his favorite brother. It was so easy to ruffle Gabe's feathers that he often forgot how much he actually loved him.

"Compromise has never been my strongest suit — yours either," Gabe said, but he relaxed as he looked at Hunter and smiled.

"True. We're a bit stubborn. But not nearly as uptight as the professor I met with," he said, instantly scowling as Becka flashed before his eyes.

"Seems like she got to you," Gabe said with a twinkle in his eyes.

Hunter still didn't want to share that he'd known her from before. Why he was so closely guarding that secret, he didn't understand. He grinned at his brother.

"Don't begin to think it's anything," Hunter warned. "The woman was so damn stiff she didn't even need a chair to sit on. All she had to do was bend her knees and there was an instant bench."

"Interesting," Gabe said.

"Don't say it like that," Hunter snapped. "It wasn't interesting. She's not my type. I don't do the uptight brainiacs. I like a much wilder woman, one who isn't afraid of a little dirt and fast times."

"How long did you speak to the professor?" Gabe asked.

"Not long, about thirty minutes. But trust me, she's *not* my type," Hunter insisted. At least she wasn't his type anymore. At one point, she'd been exactly what he'd never even known he wanted.

Her tight updo and fascinating eyes flashed before his vision. He really wanted to undo that hair, remove those glasses, and slowly unbutton her shirt ... Whoa! That was not a place his thoughts needed to be going.

"You seem awfully flustered given the woman isn't your type," Gabe pointed out.

"Just because I'm a bit curious about who she really is doesn't mean I'm interested," Hunter said with a scowl.

"Okay then, find someone else to help you," Gabe told him.

"She's smart and when she looked at the map, her eyes sparkled in the most amazing way. She wants to solve this puzzle." That was a good enough excuse to spend some time with the woman.

That sparkle in her eyes had made his groin tighten. Before he'd known what he was doing, Hunter had been leaning across the professor's desk intent on kissing those light pink lips. If she hadn't pulled back when she had, he'd have fisted his fingers into her hair and pulled her to him. He could almost taste her on his lips. Even though there had been a lot of women after Becka, none had come even remotely as close to his heart as she'd gotten.

Besides that, Hunter had always fantasized about doing it on a teacher's desk. The fantasy had always been another student, not the teacher. But Hunter had no doubt this prim professor was concealing a wild side. She was trying to hide the woman she'd once been. Why? He didn't understand.

"Where'd you go, Brother?" Gabe asked with a knowing chuckle.

"Nowhere," Hunter said too quickly before he glared at his brother. "Okay, fine, the professor intrigued me. I won't be around long enough to do anything about it anyway, and believe me when I tell you, she's not the sort of girl who wants to take a romp in the hay and then forget it happened." Maybe she'd done that once, but she wasn't going to do it again. He'd been well aware of the walls she'd put up since he'd once known her.

"Is that the only sort of girl you go out with?" Gabe asked.

"I don't go out with *any* girls. I sate the needs, then it's adios," Hunter said.

"You're proud of this?" Gabe asked with a bit of disgust.

"Damn straight I am. I don't want to get locked down, and a woman is the first step toward a noose being secured around your throat. You should be aware of that now that you've tied the knot." Hunter reached up and rubbed his neck as if that noose was already there, tightening by the second.

"I had the same attitude as you for a very long time," Gabe told him. "Meeting Josie has obviously changed that for me." Hunter wanted to mock him, but held back. "I grew up though, and now

I treat the woman I love with the respect she deserves," Gabe finished.

"Of course you do. That's all part of your stuck-up attitude," Hunter said with a chuckle.

Gabe obviously didn't find him amusing as he growled low in his throat. Hunter was impressed. He didn't think his brother had it in him to growl.

"Do you have anything to say worth speaking about?" Gabe asked.

Hunter laughed. "We're having company tonight," Hunter told him.

That made Gabe look up. "Who?"

"The professor," Hunter said as he jumped to his feet. "She'll be here in about an hour so I should probably shower so I don't smell like a mud pit."

"So it's okay to stink in front of me?" Gabe asked.

"You aren't a sexy package dying to be unwrapped," Hunter told him with a wink.

"I thought you said you weren't going there," Gabe pointed out.

"Yeah, I say a lot of things," Hunter said.

He left Gabe behind as he bounded from the den and out of the main place to one of the guesthouses. He was a little too excited about the professor's visit. Maybe he should rethink his attitude about her. They could always treasure hunt *and* warm the sheets at the same time. He was sure she could use it. He knew *he* could. Why not make the adventure a lot more fun? It wasn't like they hadn't done it before.

Hunter found himself whistling as he jumped into the large shower with jet sprays. He might just enjoy this visit home for the first time in a lot of years. And once again, it all had to do with the same woman.

Chapter Four

REBEKAH WAS UNBELIEVABLY nervous as she pulled her car up to the ranch house where she'd spent so much time when she was only eighteen years old. Why had she listened to Hunter Brannigan? Hadn't she learned years ago that she couldn't trust him? Maybe some lessons took more time than others to learn.

One thing Rebekah had known from the moment Hunter had left her office though, was that she wasn't going to be able to walk away from this. Maybe it was about the closure she desperately needed. Maybe it was her love of treasure. It was probably just her inability to walk away from a puzzle.

She'd spent the entire night researching the poem Hunter had left with her, wishing she'd had the map to go with it. But he was a smart man. He'd most likely known if she had all the pieces she wouldn't need him, and therefore wouldn't have come to the ranch.

She would have rather not come. It was messing with her head *and* her heart. But Rebekah refused to let herself go there. She was simply doing a job and she refused to allow it to be a problem. Rebekah was a reasonable person. She didn't deal in *what ifs* or *what could have beens.* She looked to what she could verify, touch, physically feel. Emotions were nothing more than a nuisance and she would push them down. When she and Hunter were done with this impossible task, she would leave and not think of him again.

Good. Now that she had her emotions under control, she felt better — or so she told herself. But as she gazed at the place where she'd thought her dreams were coming true so long ago, she knew she was a fool.

Here it was impossible for the memories not to assault her. She and Hunter had made love in so many spots on this ranch. They'd hidden in the shack on top of the hill, had snuck into his childhood bedroom where they'd tried not to make too much noise, had laid blankets down in the woods surrounding the property, had even had a midnight skinny dipping session in the creek.

She'd been free that summer — free and in love. She'd finished school doing what her parents had wanted, graduating valedictorian, getting a scholarship to one of the nicest colleges in the United States, having a one-year plan, five-year plan, and ten-year plan. She'd given up parties with friends, hadn't even gone to her senior prom. She'd graduated high school with two years of college under her belt. Her life had been all about academics and her future.

Until that summer.

It had been her one and only time to rebel and on the very first day of that new journey, she'd met Hunter Brannigan in a big way. She'd been alone, swimming in the ocean when a rogue wave had taken her down. Rebekah had feared for her life, but suddenly strong arms had wrapped around her and she'd found herself surfacing, taking in a sweet gasp of fresh air as she coughed out the seawater.

One look into Hunter's eyes and she'd been lost. He'd kissed her right then and there, in the middle of the ocean. She'd spent the entire summer with him, wrapped up in his arms and laughing like she'd never laughed before.

It had taken a few weeks before she'd had the courage to give him her virginity. Oh, but it had been spectacular. She would never forget that night. The sun had been setting, brilliant splashes of reds, oranges and purples blending together as the brightest stars became visible.

Hunter had warmed her entire body with his hands and mouth and then he'd slowly climbed up her, his lips whispering against hers as he told her how beautiful she was. Slowly, so slowly, he'd slipped inside her, and though there'd been a touch of pain, his caress and care had melted it away until all she'd felt was desire and pleasure.

She'd never wanted that night to end. And then when it had, she hadn't wanted summer to end. But of course, the fairytale had concluded, and not with a happily-ever-after. That wasn't the path Rebekah had been on then.

She would have given it all up for Hunter — *if* he'd wanted her to. But he had disappeared and she'd gone back to her real life — never allowing herself to feel so free again.

As she gazed at the place that gave her such fond memories, she felt that same ache she'd felt so long ago. Rebekah had thought that was over — had thought she'd moved on. Apparently she'd been wrong. There had been such hope inside her that he'd want her forever. She had never voiced that out loud, but the hope had been there.

She'd told no one how she felt. After all, it had been nothing more than the foolish dreams of an immature little girl. She also hadn't opened up her heart again. Her mother had warned her from a young age not to be led by her emotions. Rebekah had fully understood why when she'd dealt with the pain of losing Hunter.

And now she was agreeing to go on a treasure hunt with that same man. She must be one of those foolish women her mother had spoken of. Because the man who had stepped into her office barely resembled the person she'd fallen in love with — the carefree, loving, sweet man who had stolen her heart.

The man who had come to her the day before had been hardened, was rougher around the edges. Sure, she could still see the adventure in his eyes, but there was more to him now. Rebekah was sure she didn't want to explore what that was.

If Hunter thought she was the same young girl, then he would be unpleasantly surprised. She had grown up in the past ten years. Now she was wise, strong, and not so susceptible to a man's charms. She wouldn't fall all over herself because of a few whispered words in the dark or a few stolen kisses in the moonlight.

No. Rebekah had grown up. What surprised her was how depressed that thought made her feel. Being in this place made her want to let her hair down, made her want to run and jump in the ocean, made her want to go on those wild adventures she'd once dreamed of. Even if she allowed herself to follow this map of Hunter's, she still wouldn't fully be able to let go. She feared if she did, she'd never come back to who she needed to be.

Shaking her head to end her walk down memory lane, Rebekah stopped her car and took a big breath before she opened the door and stepped out. Her fingers clung to the strap of the computer bag wrapped around her body. The poem she'd been trying to interpret rested safely inside.

This was a business transaction, nothing more. She'd do well to remember that for the duration of her time with Hunter. She began heading to the front door when she heard noise around the corner.

What she should do was go and knock, but what she found herself doing instead was heading along the path that would lead her to the guesthouses.

The massive yard had been well taken care of, and she smiled as she closed her eyes for a moment, remembering a game of Frisbee with Hunter and his siblings that had gone on late into the night. She'd enjoyed her time alone with Hunter and she'd enjoyed time with his family. They were good people even if he wasn't, she told herself.

"I wasn't sure you'd come."

Rebekah slowly turned from her view of the property to see Hunter walking confidently toward her. The gap between them was much smaller than she would have liked. She hadn't thought it would be possible for him to be so near without her knowledge.

"You left me with little choice," she said with a bit of a scowl. "I had to return the poem to you, and … and I'm curious," she admitted.

Hunter laughed. "You never were able to turn down a challenge," he said, stopping so close to her she could practically taste him.

"There's nothing wrong with being competitive," she said with a small huff.

He looked her over and his lips turned up even higher. "Where are the glasses, Professor?"

Rebekah unconsciously fluttered her fingers as she reached for the rims. She only wore them at school. To tell the truth, she hated having the metal against her face all day. It was just that it made her appear older. Of course he would point it out.

"I only need them for reading," she lied.

He smiled bigger. She had a feeling he knew it was a mask of sorts for her. She needed to focus on anything other than Hunter Brannigan, so she found herself playing with the strap resting against her chest.

"If you're here, does that mean you want to go on an adventure with me?" he asked, clear excitement in his tone.

She felt herself stiffen. "No. I want to figure out the map, but that doesn't mean I need to actually *go* anywhere," she insisted.

"Listen Becka, it's about following the clues. You're either in or you're out. If you aren't willing to commit fully to the project then I need to find someone who is. I need to get out of here as soon as possible, so I want this puzzle solved."

He looked her deep in the eyes as he said this. He was telling her a few things with his little speech. One was that he wasn't sticking around. That hurt more than she wanted it to, though she was a fool to feel that way. He was also saying she was replaceable. Rebekah didn't like that any more than the first thing.

She narrowed her eyes and pulled her shoulders back. She knew the best thing she could do would be to walk away. Why she wasn't doing just that, she had no idea.

"I need to think a bit more about all of this before I make my final decision," she told him.

He studied her for several moments and his lips turned up again. She wasn't sure what he'd found in her expression. She didn't even know exactly what she was feeling, besides a whole lot of confusion.

"Think about the map, or think about us?" he asked.

"There is no *us*, Hunter," she snapped, her pulse accelerating.

"That's not even remotely true," he said, his eyes narrowing. Had she offended him? She didn't understand how.

The step he took toward her made her stumble backward. She wanted to stand her ground, but she absolutely didn't want him touching her. She feared what her response would be — and not that it would be bad.

"You can't possibly be afraid of me," he said, not backing away.

"Of course I'm not afraid of you, Hunter. I just prefer to stay on task," she said. "There's really no point in discussing things that are better left buried in the past."

"Dang, you have that professor voice down pat, don't you?" he said with a chuckle.

Rebekah's fingers tightened on the strap she was clutching like a lifeline. He had come to her for help, but he certainly wasn't interested in making things the least bit easy on her.

"I want to talk rules before I even *consider* doing this with you, Hunter," she told him.

That made his lips turn up even more. She didn't appreciate the fact that he was so amused by her. She was no longer that naïve little teenager she'd been when he'd rescued her from the ocean.

"Rules?" he finally said.

"Yes, rules, Hunter," she stiffly told him. "You came to me wanting help, and now I'm telling you my terms."

"I've never been too good at following rules," he informed her.

"I shouldn't have come. This wasn't wise," she said, the stress of being there beginning to weigh on her.

Before she could so much as move an inch, Hunter reached out, taking her hand. "Sometimes in life, the biggest mistakes turn out to be the greatest blessings," he said quietly.

The husky timber of his voice and the fire in his eyes had her knees shaking. Was he saying what they'd once shared had been a mistake? Or was he saying that doing this treasure hunt together would end up being a blessing? Rebekah really didn't know.

With concentrated effort she pulled her hand from his grip and took a step back as she tried to get her breathing under control. This was wrong — it was so wrong, but she couldn't seem to force herself to walk away from it.

"Can you do this professionally or are we going to have problems?" she asked.

"I don't see any problem with us working together," he told her, but the look in his eyes promised the opposite.

"Fine, then do you want to hear my terms?" she pushed.

He smiled at her, as a parent would while indulging a naughty child. She decided she would just have to get used to that from him. She couldn't nitpick at everything.

"What are your terms?" he asked.

"There will be no touching, no flirting, no trying to get in my pants," she began. His smile grew, but he said nothing. She took a breath and continued.

"We will keep this strictly business. And if you can't promise this, then I'm not helping you." She crossed her arms and gave him her sternest look. His smile grew and though she wanted to keep on talking to fill the uncomfortable silence, she waited.

"Let me counter," he told her. The low timbre of his voice made her tremble. "I promise not to do anything you don't want."

She waited for him to go on, but he'd decided that was all he wanted to say. She glared at him for several moments but it seemed that no matter how stern a look she gave him, he wasn't one to back down.

"Then I guess there's not a problem because I think I've made myself clear. I want *nothing* from you," she said.

"Then we're ready to begin," he told her. She knew this was going to end up badly for her, but she was now too committed to back away. She sighed before deciding to give it a try.

"Let's look at the map," she told him.

Hunter looked as if he wanted to say something, but then much to her relief he let out a sigh and began walking back to the guesthouse. She followed behind him, her fingers aching from gripping the strap on her chest so tightly.

As they stepped into the small cabin and Rebekah looked around, memories of the past assaulted her. She wondered how truly professional she was going to be able to remain.

This wasn't just anyone, it was Hunter, her first love. The past should have been kept buried, but it appeared she had just been provided a shovel to dig it all back up.

Chapter Five

HUNTER WIPED HIS palms on his pants, shocked to realize they were sweating. He had been in places where bullets zipped past him, nearly taking his life, and he hadn't felt as nervous as he did while Becka sat across from him.

What was it about this particular girl? He wasn't sure. They'd had one incredible summer together and then he hadn't seen her again until he'd stepped into her stuffy office at the college. But he'd thought about her over the years. He'd left women's beds and gone to sleep with a vision of Becka hiding behind his closed eyelids.

There had been something special about her that long ago summer, and time had only added to her appeal. He hoped like hell she'd be washed from his system by the time they came to whatever end his father had planned for him with this treasure hunt.

"I got the original map from my father after his passing. I had to leave for an assignment right away. When I got back I went through the box and looked at the rest of the clues within," Hunter said as he pushed the materials toward Becka.

"What is all of this?" she asked.

"I don't exactly know. There are some documents that might help us follow the map, and the poem has clues in it as well, though I have no idea what my dad was thinking," he told her.

"Did he treasure hunt?" she asked.

"Not that I know of. He liked adventure, that's for sure," he said with a chuckle. "I always liked that about the old man."

"Sometimes a sense of adventure can be hard on a family," she pointed out.

"Look, I don't have some sob story about my family. We grew up, parted ways and each of us went on with our lives, but we're happy. We talk once in a while and we do our own thing," he said, instantly defensive.

"I wasn't trying to imply there was anything wrong with your family," she told him with a frown.

"I just find this situation ridiculous. I have things to do," he said.

"Like what?" She looked up at him, curiosity in her eyes.

"What do you mean?" he asked hesitantly.

"What do you have to do that's more important than your father's last wishes?" she pushed.

Hunter's chair scraped back as he stood up from the table and moved to the fridge. He was restless, and it was showing. He didn't like to be stuck in one place for too long and this quest made him feel trapped. There was no way the uptight professor could even begin to understand that.

"I take pictures," he said. She raised a brow. "I document events — war, natural disasters, poverty, things that most people don't see unless they open a magazine."

"Your father's wishes are certainly important, but I can see why you want to get back to your job. It's actually pretty awesome," she said. The awe in her tone made his chest puff out the slightest bit.

"Yeah, I like what I do," he admitted.

"So just look at this like it's one more adventure. You can document it with your camera. I don't think the treasure hunt is going to be easy or the puzzle solved in a day, so you might as well quit fighting it and start looking at the good in the situation."

He drank a long swallow of his beer before he smiled at her. Hunter remembered how upbeat she'd been that summer ten years before, and though her unfortunate clothing was a lot different now, it seemed there was still a sense of adventure residing deep inside her. Maybe the treasure would be in bringing that out in her. But that would just be for him. His father didn't know of his relationship with Becka. How the old man had gotten her name, he might never know.

"I can't seem to find any clues in the poem," she told him, bringing him out of his thoughts.

"Read it out loud and we'll go from there," he suggested.

She grabbed the paper and the light of excitement in her eyes was enough to make his heart beat just a little bit faster. He might be complaining about the treasure hunt, but at the same time he wasn't too upset over doing it with her. Becka began the poem and he was mesmerized.

The thing you seek is neither near nor far,
But to find it, you will have to search
Places both new and old

"What does that mean?" he asked.

"Let me finish without interruption," she scolded, which made him smile. He zipped his lips closed.

There's more to life than what money can buy,
And wisdom comes from up high.
Trust me to guide you in the right direction
Then a treasure untold will be your blessing.
This place I've found is not hidden,
But trails and peaks are a given.
Remember your roots so you might find
A heart that is full of peace of mind.
Ending where it all began is a must,
But beginning where it ended might be your first stand.
Go to where you felt the most peace

And then you will find what the earth can't keep.
There might be fire,
And there might be water,
But trails to follow are surely shallow.
But be careful of the perils along the way,
For this journey isn't for the weak of heart,
Not for the faint of mind.
Ask for help, don't be afraid
And in the end you will surely find
A peaceful heart and a blessed mind.
I am always with you,
My love never ending,
Come back home son
To the beginning.

Hunter was quiet as Becka finished the poem, then looked at him as if he had any answers at all as to what it meant. *Go back to the beginning?* The beginning of what?

"I really don't know," he finally said.

"Is there a special place around here that might trigger a memory?" she asked.

Most of the special places Hunter could think of at the ranch were connected to Becka, but again, that wasn't something his father would have known anything about. He was lost. Maybe it had to do with places he'd been with his brothers. It might not have anything at all to do with Becka. He was confused.

"Let's pull the rest of the items out and maybe then I will get a clue," he told her.

They did just that and over the next few hours, the pair studied the map, the poem, and some miscellaneous documents his father had thrown together. None of it made much sense. But one place was coming to mind as he searched through it all.

"I think it's this ghost town we once visited," he suggested. "We can go tomorrow."

He didn't want to go there — not with Becka — not without the surety of them going back in time and letting it all go. Hunter wasn't sure of anything at the moment, especially her surrender to him.

"Tomorrow won't work for me. I have classes all day. We can go the day after."

He didn't want to let her leave, and that made no sense to him. But he would do what had to be done. That was his father's wish.

"Okay, then we will get started then," he finally said. There wasn't much of a choice beyond that.

"We'll go the day after tomorrow then," she said after a long pause. "But this might be nothing more than a wild goose chase."

He looked at her for a long moment, wondering if that's exactly what it was. It didn't matter because it wasn't something he could turn away from.

"I know."

Hunter found himself unable to do much more talking after that. Even after Becka left and he was alone with his thoughts, he wasn't sure of what he was going to do. He did know he would try to finish this hunt though, even if there wasn't a pot of gold at the end of the rainbow.

Chapter Six

REBEKAH TOLD HERSELF that she just had to continue breathing in and out. If she took this project one day at a time instead of looking at it as one long adventure, then she was going to do much better.

Even telling herself all of this didn't truly help though. Being in the same room with Hunter Brannigan for long periods of time was messing with her head and heart in a way she hadn't known was still possible. And she didn't like it one little bit. She'd barely been able to concentrate during her classes and somehow she found herself wandering, missing Hunter already. It was ridiculous.

Exhaustion filled her as she strolled into an old restaurant she'd once ate at with Hunter. Being with Hunter the day before hadn't been easy on her emotions. But as she looked up and found an old friend standing at the hostess station, she found a smile lifting her lips.

"Aimee, is that you?" Rebekah asked, making the woman look up.

"Becka?" She looked confused for a moment, then she let out a squeal and ran toward Rebekah. "It's been so long."

Aimee threw her arms around Rebekah and the two women hugged, ignoring the people waiting nearby with curious looks on their faces.

"I can't believe you haven't been back to see me," Aimee said with a pout as she pulled back.

"I'm sorry. I sort of ran from here," Rebekah admitted.

"I know you did, but I've missed you," Aimee told her. "And do you realize where you're standing?"

That confused Rebekah. "In the Surf and Sip restaurant?" she told her. "The name has changed, but we ate here often that summer ten years ago."

"That's because it's now *my* place," Aimee told her.

"You own it?"

"Yep, for three years now. And it's doing amazing. It's fate that you're back here," Aimee said.

"I feel like such a terrible person that I didn't stay in contact," Rebekah said, feeling shame.

"I could hold it over your head, but as long as you promise not to disappear on me again, then I might think about forgiving you," Aimee said.

"Can you join me for dinner and we'll catch up?" Rebekah asked.

"Yes! I'll get you a table and finish up what I'm doing. Give me about thirty minutes," Aimee told her before leading her inside the main room.

"It's beautiful in here," Rebekah told her.

"Thank you. I'm a little proud." She then turned toward the hovering waiter. "We have a special guest tonight. Give her anything she wants."

"Don't be intimidated by her. I'm low maintenance," Rebekah assured the man.

"Wine?" Aimee asked, and the waiter handed over a menu.

"If I remember correctly, the lady enjoys a nice glass of Dom Perignon," a deep male voice said from behind them, making a shiver run down Rebekah's spine. Slowly, she turned and found her gaze locked with a seemingly amused Hunter. "She likes to bathe in it too, if I remember correctly," he added, making Rebekah want to climb beneath the table as images of Hunter pouring champagne over her breasts flashed before her eyes.

Hunter had brought out the champagne and they'd sipped it and poured it on each other a lot that summer. It had been her first taste of alcohol and she had very much enjoyed the sparkly drink that had left her slightly light-headed.

"Of course, Mr. Brannigan," the waiter said, keeping a professional mask in place before he turned to go and get the expensive champagne.

"I don't need that," Rebekah tried to call out, but it was too late.

"Live a little," Aimee said with a smile as she turned her head to look back and forth between her and Hunter. The restaurant might as well have been empty as alone as she suddenly felt with the man she'd been running from.

"Are you making my help run for you?" Aimee said before she leaned in and gave Hunter a side hug. "You haven't been here in so long I was beginning to get my feelings hurt."

"I was here three days ago," Hunter told her.

"Yeah, but you'll disappear again soon," she pointed out.

Rebekah watched their easy banter and felt a slight stirring of jealousy. Not of Aimee, but of how easy it was for the two of them to speak together. Of course, they hadn't been lovers, not that Rebekah was aware of.

"But for now, I'm craving pasta," he told her.

"Mmm, go with the pasta primavera. The cook made a special sauce that's amazing," Aimee suggested.

"As long as you hurry back to join me," Rebekah said, a bit of desperation in her tone. She was now avoiding looking into Hunter's eyes.

"I will hurry back, but I'm sure Hunter will be more than happy to keep you company in the meantime," Aimee said.

Rebekah wanted to call the woman a traitor, but since she hadn't bothered to come back and see the girl who had once been a great friend, she knew she had no right to talk. Aimee turned and left, leaving her standing there with Hunter. She didn't even want to sit. She was trying to decide if she should turn and walk away. Feeling awkward, Rebekah finally did sit, and Hunter smiled before taking the seat across from her.

"That summer so long ago, you and Aimee were pretty close," Hunter pointed out.

"Yes, we were. She was a great friend." She sighed. "You don't need to sit here and eat with me. I'm fine with being alone," she added.

"I want to sit here with you." The smile he gave her was enough to make her fall to her butt, if she weren't already on it. The waiter returned with the bottle of Dom and Hunter took it from him. "I'll pour." The man left and he filled both their glasses.

"Thank you," she murmured, picking up the glass and taking a big gulp.

"I have a suggestion," he told her with a wink. "Why don't we play a little game?"

The champagne flavor was perfection, but it took her back to that cabin in the woods on his property, to how he'd poured it over her stomach before he'd ran his tongue along the curve of her hip and up and over her breasts. Her breathing weakened as she tried pulling herself back into the present.

"What are you talking about?" she asked, hating the slight huskiness in her voice.

"If we're going to solve this puzzle, we're going to have to spend time together. Let's see if we can get through a single meal," he said.

"That's a game?" she asked.

"*Life* is a game," he told her with a smile before he sipped again while his eyes trailed down to the V of her neck. That made her breathing deepen a bit more.

"I don't believe that," she said sadly.

That summer so long ago had been about fun and games. But she'd left that summer and chosen to be responsible, to do what she had to do. Her life was no longer about playing. It was about being an adult.

"So you aren't willing to bend at all?" he asked, challenge in his eyes.

That made her hackles rise. He was challenging her, and it wasn't easy for her to walk away from a challenge.

"I can sit here and behave," she told him, lifting her glass only to realize it was empty. She'd polished that off way too quickly. Still, she didn't complain when Hunter reached out and refilled the glass. Maybe it would take the edge off.

"To mutual understanding," Hunter said as he lifted his glass. She only hesitated a moment before she clinked hers against his, almost feeling as if she were making a deal with the devil.

Hunter leaned a bit closer to her and Rebekah felt that urge to run again, but at the same time she wasn't sure if she wanted to run to him or away from him. It was killing her not knowing what to do.

"I forgot to mention right away how much I like that dress you're wearing," he said, his eyes caressing every inch of skin that showed above the table. "I wouldn't mind peeling it away inch by beautiful inch."

Rebekah coughed as her drink went down wrong. Hunter wasn't playing nice at all. That sultry edge to his voice made her feel like there was no one else in the room but the two of them, and it made her thighs quiver. He'd done that to her when she was young, but her innocence had been an excuse then.

She wasn't that innocent little girl anymore. She should be able to tell him to stop acting like a fool, then stand up and walk out of the room — preferably *after* throwing her champagne in his face. But her legs wouldn't carry her anywhere at this particular moment, unless it was straight into his arms.

Hunter was a skilled man in more ways than one. And he was melting her. She would be damned before she told him any of that. The waiter returned, saving Rebekah from having to respond to him.

"Have you decided what you would like to eat?" the man asked as he held his tablet.

Rebekah couldn't open her mouth to speak. Hunter stepped in for both of them. For once she was a bit thankful.

"We're both going to have the pasta primavera and salads with house dressing. Stuffed mushrooms for an appetizer, and the house-made bread, please."

The waiter left quickly and Rebekah found her gaze captured by Hunter's once more. She wasn't this meek little woman and she hated that she felt that way.

"So you obviously stayed in contact with Aimee over the years," Rebekah finally said. If she could keep the conversation off the two of them then her life would be a lot easier.

"I haven't been to town much, but we've kept in contact with email. She's a fan of my work and has a beautiful little girl."

"She has a daughter?" Now Rebekah felt terrible.

"A picturesque girl. I met her the other day and she was all smiles."

"That's wonderful," Rebekah said, meaning it.

"Yeah, I wouldn't mind a few like her, but that would require me staying in one place for longer than a couple weeks," he told her with a laugh.

His words shocked her. Rebekah didn't know how to respond. She decided it was nothing more than words.

"You've always been too adventurous to settle down and have kids," she said.

Rebekah felt herself having a difficult time thinking when he gazed at her with that soulful look in his eyes. She knew he wasn't thinking of having those children with her, but the seed had been planted and she desperately wanted to uproot it.

"I do love adventure," he admitted. "Which is why we're going to have fun on this treasure hunt. I think you want some thrills of your own. You are trying to hide it, but the more I look into your eyes, the more I see how much you want it."

"Maybe I do want to do something I haven't done before," she said almost defiantly. "That doesn't mean I don't love what I do, or my day-to-day life."

"So you've come to me for adventure?"

"*You* came to *me*," she pointed out.

"But *you* chose to stay," he said with such intensity she felt glued to her seat.

The waiter set down the bread, salads and mushrooms before quickly disappearing again. The interruption gave her a moment to compose herself.

"I did choose to stay, Hunter, because I'm intrigued. It has nothing to do with wanting to seek adventure, and it really doesn't have anything to do with wanting to spend time with you," she told him.

Pushing away her nerves, she lifted her fork, forced herself to spear some lettuce and tomato, and took a bite. She was sure it tasted amazing, but she could barely chew and swallow, let alone enjoy it.

"I think you're protesting a lot," Hunter said, his posture lazy, his eyes crinkled as he smiled before taking a bite of his food and sighing. "I always have enjoyed a great meal."

That comment made her look down his chest to his flat stomach. The man might eat whatever he wanted, but he was so damn active he was unbelievably beautiful. She hated that every single thing he was saying was making her think of something else.

"I came here to hunt for treasure. That is all. Don't try to read more into it," she snapped.

For the first time that evening, Hunter's eyes narrowed and she could see he was trying to control a brewing temper. He leaned toward her and Rebekah knew she should retreat. She was glued to the spot though, unable to do a thing about it.

"You don't have to fight it, Becka," he finally said, his temper evaporating as quickly as it had arisen.

"I'm not a complicated person, Hunter. I do things by the book and I don't stray."

"You allowed yourself to let go ten years ago," he pointed out.

"That was a long time ago and in a different lifetime. Don't try to find that girl. She's long gone," she warned.

"There are people who sit on the sidelines and those who won't allow life to pass them by. I choose to live my life, not stand by and watch it pass me. We might only have spent one summer together, but I saw the adventure inside you, and I know it's still there. Don't run and hide, Becka."

Surprisingly, Rebekah found herself smiling. "Is that a speech you practice?" she asked. Maybe it was the champagne, and maybe he was just wearing her down. She wasn't sure what it was, but the tenseness was fading and she found herself actually enjoying their sparring.

"Well then, let the adventure begin," she said. She saw the happy surprise in his eyes and was glad she had decided to let go a bit.

"Good. If you don't allow yourself to let go once in a while, you'll wake up one day realizing you never had a chance to live," he told her.

"I've lived. Just because my way of life might not suit everyone doesn't mean it's wrong," she pointed out.

"Would it have made a difference ten years ago if I would have came to you, stolen you away to some remote island, and held you captive?" he asked.

Rebekah gripped her glass so tightly she was surprised it didn't shatter. She couldn't look away from the intensity of his eyes as he waited for her to give him an answer she didn't have. She wanted to tell him it wouldn't have made a difference but she wasn't sure. She definitely didn't want to tell him that.

"It doesn't matter because that didn't happen and I don't believe in wishing or thinking of what could have been. That's useless emotion," she said.

"Maybe," he agreed. "But sometimes if you don't think of the past or the future, the present doesn't matter."

Rebekah sat across from him as he put all these thoughts she didn't want into her head. She was wondering if her body would still slide perfectly against his, if he would kiss his way down her shoulders, cup her breasts, whisper into her ears causing shudders to roll through her system. She wondered if it would feel differently, or if she would respond the same way.

The fire in Hunter's eyes as he sat across from her left her with no doubt: He knew what she was thinking about. He'd said he wanted to play a game — and it was a game she was losing. But she had made it through the meal; she'd survived. Maybe her body was a quivering mass, and maybe she was a bit stuck in the past, but she had survived the meal.

The waiter brought out coffee with dessert and she gratefully sipped it, needing to clear her head as Hunter stayed abnormally quiet.

"We have a long day tomorrow, Hunter. I think we can call the night good," she finally told him.

He smiled at her, that secret smile of his that made her want to demand to know what was going through his mind. But she wouldn't ask. When he rose, she tried to do the same, but her knees were shaking. She found him leaning over her as she tried to tell herself to breathe.

"Get plenty of rest, Becka." His voice was soft as his breath caressed her face.

"I can take care of myself," she told him. He leaned a bit closer and she had to fight the urge not to close the space between them and run her lips against his.

"I'm a gentleman. I don't mind taking care of you," he told her before reaching up and caressing her cheek with his rough finger.

"I need to go, Hunter," she said, her words barely above a whisper.

"I'll walk you out," he told her.

"I'm capable of doing that on my own, too," she informed him, a bit of strength creeping back into her voice.

He smiled. "I'm a gentleman, remember?" he reminded her before standing up and holding out his hand.

With reluctance, Rebekah took it and let him help her up. It wasn't until they were outside that she realized Aimee hadn't come back to the table. Her old friend was a traitor. Rebekah would call her on it very soon.

When they made it outside, the streets were empty and quiet as he walked her to her car about a block away. She didn't know what to say as her arm rested in his, sending warmth through her. She was mostly relieved when they reached her car. She didn't want to leave him, which told her she should get away and re-group.

"Thank you for dinner," she said, since he'd paid the check before she'd been able to argue.

Hunter said nothing as he turned her body so she was facing him, then ran a hand through her hair and tugged, pulling her close to him.

"We can't do this, it's breaking the rules," she warned. But she didn't pull away from him like she should have.

"To hell with the rules. This is something we owe each other," he countered. The desire in his voice made her melt as he pulled her closer to him, her breasts brushing against his chest.

His tone was filled with desire and his touch was anything but gentle. And she loved it, though she was afraid to admit that even to herself. Without waiting any longer, his lips touched hers and fire spread through her system.

She sighed against his mouth, opening to him as his tongue sought entrance. The hand cupped in her hair, tugged, and his other hand ran down her back to rest on the curve of her butt. Hunger, unlike anything she could remember, flooded through her. She was drowning in his arms and she didn't want to come up for air.

His scent of woodsy spice surrounded her, making her cling to him even more tightly as she got lost in his arms. It was the same smell that had mesmerized her so many years before. The sea pounded in the background, the only noise in their private cocoon.

His tongue tasted hers, and she didn't resist the pull of him. He was so hot, so familiar, and for this moment she was as lost as she'd once been in his embrace. When Hunter pulled back, she whimpered. She opened her eyes and saw fierce desire staring back at her.

And it scared her. This couldn't happen. Panic seeped in, and then he released her and took a step back. He opened his mouth before he closed it again. Then he took another step back and sighed.

"Get some rest," he told her. And then he turned and walked away. Rebekah watched him until he was out of her sight.

Only then did she slip into her car, where she leaned her head against the steering wheel. She wasn't sure of anything at this moment — especially herself. She just knew she'd bitten off far more than she was capable of chewing.

Chapter Seven

NERVES ASKEW, REBEKAH stood next to the large building at the airfield and watched Hunter loading gear into a small airplane. His mussed hair was blowing in the breeze as a seagull dive-bombed him. Hunter swatted the bird away and then his lips turned up in a breathtaking smile that had her heart skipping a beat.

Rebekah knew she was in some serious trouble as she gazed at her first love while he stood at the sleek private plane wearing only a pair of khaki shorts and a fitted T-shirt. His muscles rippled in the rays of the sun as he lifted his arms and stretched. Beautiful. He was pure beauty, causing an unbelievable ache in her stomach as she tried reminding herself she'd made a good decision ten years before, and a not-so-good decision in coming on this quest with him.

On the other hand, it never hurt to take in some eye candy, did it? It was a natural response for any woman presented with so much bronze and steel. As she stood there gazing at him, she tried to think like the professor she was and simply appreciate the exquisiteness of a beautiful man.

Logic always worked for her, and she was going to give herself a break and give herself an out at the same time. With a deep breath, she began walking across the pavement to where he was stowing the last items in the plane.

An F-18 flew overhead and he gazed up at the sky, his profile brilliant as his expression changed to that of an excited child. Boys and fast toys were something she never had been able to truly understand.

Even as he watched the speeding jet she saw the restlessness in his body. Even ten years before he'd been a young man on a mission — too excited about life to sit still. It was something she envied about him. He followed his dreams and he didn't apologize for it. She wished she had the same courage.

Though Rebekah was quiet as she approached him, he turned and gave her an intense glance as he shifted to give her his full attention.

"You're right on time," he said. The deep baritone of his voice sent a shiver through her. She looked from him to the small plane and wondered how she was going to survive the ride.

"I don't like to be late," she responded as he walked her around to the passenger side of the plane and pulled open the door. He held out his hand and the contact sent a sizzle through her as he helped her onboard.

He didn't say anything before shutting the door and moving around to the other side, then climbing in. There wasn't a barrier between them, and his strong thigh pressed against hers as he got comfortable.

"Do you need help with the seat belt?" he asked as she sat still in the seat, afraid to move an inch, which would cause their clothed thighs to rub together.

"I think I can manage a clasp," she said with a nervous chuckle.

"You aren't afraid of flying are you?" he asked as if that would be unheard of.

"No. Not at all," she said. It wasn't the flying she was nervous about. It was the close proximity.

"Good. It's a great day to be in the skies. The wind is calm and the skies are clear. We aren't going too far."

"Where exactly are we going? You didn't say much about it," she pointed out.

"I think I know the first clue. It's in Bodie California, an old mining town that the state parks have taken over. My father had a sense of humor, I'm finding out," he said with a chuckle. "The place is located in the Basin Range of the Eastern Sierra Nevada Mountains, about thirteen miles east of Highway 395."

"Why would there be a clue there?" she asked, as her trembling fingers failed to attach the seatbelt after all.

He reached over and did it for her and as his fingers trailed across her stomach, she found herself holding her breath. His intoxicating fragrance surrounded her in the closed plane, and with his hands on her at the same time, she worried for her sanity.

"I can't figure out the clues. In fact, I don't understand why he's having me do this at all. I remember when I was young, he took me through the town and he was excited. Something in the clues made me think this was where we need to start. I might be wrong, but we'll see."

Rebekah felt the desire in him to get going — to be doing anything other than standing still — or sitting, in their case. He carefully went through his pre-flight checklist and then started the plane and soon they were taxiing out to the runway.

As they lifted off into the sky, Rebekah felt elation filling her, taking away her nerves from being pressed against his side. She loved to fly, hadn't done it on a private plane in a long time, but there was definitely a freedom in this adventure that she hadn't even known she'd been longing for. It wasn't until her cheeks were getting sore that she realized she was grinning widely.

"I can see you're enjoying this," Hunter told her with a grin of his own.

Their eyes connected and she felt the intense pull that made her want to lean over and run her lips across his solid jaw. It took several moments before she was able to turn away. They'd barely begun their day and already it was too much. She had better do her best to keep herself under control.

Focusing her gaze out the window, she looked down at the land below them, watching as they made their way out of the city. Other planes could be seen in the distance, but still, she felt like it was only the two of them, that the rest of the world had fallen away. She enjoyed that feeling a bit too much.

The sun beat through the protected windshield, warming her skin to the point of being uncomfortable. She was already overheated just from being in the presence of Hunter. The flight should only take about an hour, but she feared it might be the longest hour of her life. Then they would have to make the return trip on top of it.

Hunter flew the plane perfectly, and Rebekah sat still in her seat, not making a sound. No turbulence interrupted their flight and she had to appreciate the skill the man next to her had. He was good at anything he wanted to do.

When Hunter had made the proposition of treasure hunting to her, she'd been leery, but the excitement in her gut told her that no matter how cautious she tried to be, she was excited. She might never be Lara Croft, but this would be a small taste of it. She could endure her raging hormones, she assured herself.

Rebekah found herself relaxing as they continued to fly, and before she knew it, she was pressed against Hunter's side instead of straining against the door, trying unsuccessfully to get away from him.

Turning her head was a bad idea, because his eyes were only inches from hers, and even worse, his lips were right there — right in kissing distance. Without thought, she licked her dry lips and his eyes sparked, making that dip in her stomach ache in an almost unbearable way.

"I'm ready when you are," he said in a throaty drawl.

Where was her Lara Croft persona when she needed it? That woman would lean into him, kiss him the way she wanted to, and damn the consequences. But instead of doing what her body craved with an unquenchable need, she pulled back from Hunter.

"How much longer?" she asked.

Hunter grinned at her, making her desire him that much more. She wished he'd get angry, or give up on her. That would make their time together easier. With him being charming, she wasn't sure she'd be able to resist what she knew he was more than willing to offer.

One thing Rebekah knew beyond a doubt was that she wasn't in her stuffy office back at the college. She also wasn't in the auditorium giving a lecture the kids didn't want to hear. She was on an epic adventure and she wasn't going to waste it. She needed this more than she feared her feelings of Hunter.

She decided she wasn't going to think anymore about the kiss she and Hunter had shared, and she wasn't going to keep thinking about sharing another one with him. She certainly wasn't going to imagine climbing up onto his lap, trailing her lips down his solid jaw and ripping his shirt open with her teeth. No. Those thoughts weren't going to be on her mind at all.

Turning to look out her window, Rebekah enjoyed the feel of the sun on her cheeks and focused on the ground as Hunter began descending. Never had she been so grateful to quit flying. Normally, she loved every single moment of the freedom of being in the sky.

"Are you enjoying getting out of the classroom?" Hunter asked.

They'd been so silent for the past several minutes that the sound of his voice made her jump. She turned to see the smile that put on his face. Calming her nerves, she decided to be honest.

"Yes, very much. Don't get me wrong, I love being a professor. I knew from a young age that I would go to college and I'd do something that would matter, something that would affect the lives of others. But sometimes it's a bit confining," she admitted.

"I would rather die than be locked down to a desk," he told her.

"Yes, I believe that," she said with a chuckle.

"Hey, I can be responsible, but why should I be stuck at a desk night and day when instead I can be outdoors, on a new adventure every week?"

"There's nothing wrong with that. We need people like you in the world. But there also has to be people like me. It's why we all have a love of different things," she said, a bit too sadly.

"You might like teaching, but there's adventure in your soul. You weren't meant to be locked down," he said wisely.

Rebekah wasn't sure she liked that he seemed to know her so damn well. They'd only spent one summer together, and that had been ten years ago. She'd barely been out of high school. And she'd never once told anyone of her desire to travel and seek adventure. But arguing would do her no good.

"The outdoors is great in good weather. Not so much when the weather turns," she pointed out.

"Yes, it all depends on where you're at," he said with a wink. "I've been in Antarctic conditions where pieces of my body sadly disappeared, and also on peaceful islands in the dead of winter where I swam naked and laid out on the beach for hours."

Her cheeks instantly heating, Rebekah sent him a stern look. "Some of us would worry about people taking pictures."

"I have nothing to hide," he told her with a hearty laugh.

The images flooding her mind of him wet and naked, his muscles gleaming, his body … Rebekah put a halt to those thoughts before they could grow any further out of control. She was stuck in a small plane with him. She certainly didn't want to be picturing him in the nude.

"It has to get lonely in the middle of nowhere without a soul in sight. I would be a bit freaked out," she said.

"It's heaven. Not something I would want to do forever, but after a particularly bad assignment sometimes I just need to get away from it all."

There was a slight tightness in his voice as he said that and she wondered if some of the bad he'd witnessed weighed on him. She wanted to ask, but she wasn't anything to him. She didn't have the right.

"I'm sorry," she told him.

"Nothing to be sorry about," he told her with a careless shrug. "I clear my head and then I'm on to my next big adventure. It's great."

In the blink of an eye Hunter was able to brush off that tightness. She wished she were able to do the same. Maybe it was a male thing. She wasn't sure.

"You've changed quite a bit in ten years," Hunter pointed out.

Rebekah sighed. "I grew up," she said.

"Did you ever think about the two of us?"

That question shocked Rebekah. She hadn't been expecting it, hadn't come up with an answer if asked. A nervous sweat broke out on her brow. It wasn't something she could outright lie about.

"It's not something I dwelled on," she finally said. "But I won't lie and say that meeting you and spending that summer with you wasn't something that shaped me. It's over though."

Not knowing what to expect, Rebekah was again shocked when Hunter laughed. She couldn't help but look over into his sparkling eyes.

"You need to get out of the classroom a little more, Professor. Life can't be so easily summarized or placed in a box. And our time together is most certainly worth thinking about a lot more than once in a while."

"You're incredibly full of yourself," she said.

"I have no reason not to be," he assured her.

She considered her response for several heartbeats before replying to him again. The ground was growing ever closer and she popped her ears as they neared the runway. The sooner they were out of the plane, the sooner this reminiscence about the past would be over.

"We all have faults, Hunter. I think a person is much more impressive who admits to them."

His laughter died away as he glanced at her before focusing again on the instruments in front of him. He looked serious all of a sudden and she almost wished for the light-heartedness of just a moment before.

"I don't think we have faults. I think we have characteristics that shape us. Nothing we do is right or wrong, it is just the way it is," he said.

"Maybe," she said with hesitation. "But there are turns in my life I would change if I could go back."

He raised a brow at her. "Am I one of those turns?"

Rebekah couldn't look away from him as he smoothly landed the plane and began taxiing it toward the private hangar where she could see a shiny black SUV waiting. He said nothing else as he waited for her answer. She could lie to him, maybe end all this suffering she was feeling. But for some reason she didn't want to taint that memory.

"No, Hunter. That was a critical part of my growing up," she finally told him.

He stopped the plane and shifted, pressing himself even more closely to her. He looked as if he was going to kiss her again, and Rebekah found herself hoping he would. The inconsistency of her emotions was too insane for her to try to figure out.

"Maybe we aren't done growing," he said.

Rebekah was lost in his gaze. She was lost in it all. And she wasn't entirely sure she wanted to be found.

Chapter Eight

*T*HE PLANE RIDE had been both exhilarating and torturous for Hunter. Having Becka pressed against his side for an hour had felt right, but had made him want to press her down into the seats in a horizontal way.

He was rock solid in his pants as he jumped from the plane, then held out a hand to assist Becka down. She looked at his fingers as if they were snakes, then climbed down on her own, refusing his help. That might be a good idea at this particular moment. With his hormones raging, he wasn't sure he wouldn't press her up against the metal of his plane and ravage her right then and there in the very public airport.

He felt like a rowdy teenager who had been chasing the girl for too long. What made the situation even worse was the kiss they'd shared the night before. It had awoken every cell of his body, and he had images flashing through his mind of the two of them twined together as she called out his name in ecstasy. They'd been great together. He imagined they'd be even better now.

When he stepped back from the plane, Becka reached inside and grabbed her backpack, clutching it in her fingers, her knuckles white as she held on tightly. To fight these feelings was insane for both of them, but he didn't see another option.

Hunter had no doubt Becka was feeling as much as he was, but for some strange reason he didn't understand, she didn't want to do anything about it. It wasn't as if either of them was in a relationship. He didn't see what it would hurt for them to ease the strain they were both under. But Hunter had never really understood women.

Hunter grabbed what he needed from the plane and led Becka to the awaiting vehicle. He thanked the man who'd dropped it off and then it was just the two of them once more. Maybe he should have hired a driver instead. It might have been a safer option.

That thought made Hunter smile. He never had been one of those men to choose the safest route. He didn't see a reason to do so now. Becka sat in the passenger seat as she studied the map sitting on her lap.

"I don't see how this is leading us to Bodie," she said.

"Do you see that mark there?" he asked her, pointing at a spot on the map, the beginning of their journey.

"Yes," she said, her brows furrowed.

"That's a grave marker. It's been a long time since I've been to Bodie, but I believe that's the cemetery there and we'll find whatever clue was left behind if we go," he told her.

She gazed at the map a while longer and then smiled. "I hope so. If this isn't it, we're not going to know what to do."

"Why would my father lead me on a treasure hunt that I had no chance of figuring out?" he asked.

"Why would he put *my* name to help you?" she responded. "It doesn't seem that I'm helping at all."

"We just have to keep following the clues and we can get it all figured out."

"I guess so," she said, with little confidence.

Becka put the map away as they began making the sixty mile drive to the ghost town. The farther they got from the Mammoth Yosemite Airport, the more secluded they became. There were a few cars here and there, but not as many tourists as he would have expected — even in the beginning of winter.

As they reached the outskirts of town, Hunter looked over as a slight tremor ran through Becka.

"Are you okay?" he asked.

She turned and gave him a brilliant smile that made his muscles tense. Damn, she was beautiful. It was nerve-wracking how much so.

"Do you realize you were the first person to give me a real adventure?" she said, surprising him.

"Today?" he asked.

"No, ten years ago. I'd been studious and responsible until that summer and for a few short months, I got lost in the fun of living life. I just realized that I've been locked away again, in college learning and now teaching. So I guess you're the one to give me another adventure," she said.

"I could give you a lot more," he promised her. He wanted to pull the vehicle over and show her exactly what he was talking about. Instead of the shutters going back into place, she smiled.

"I'm good," she told him.

"Yes you are," he readily agreed.

"Tell me about this place," she insisted as she gazed out the windows, seeing their destination quickly approaching. Hunter would rather talk about the two of them, but he had time. He hoped for the first time in a while that this adventure would last for a bit. He wasn't in a hurry to leave and find a new place. That was strange for him.

"In the late eighteen hundreds the town was said to have been nearly a mile long, which was huge for the time. But then a disastrous fire happened, wiping out a lot of it. Forty years later another fire further devastated the place. What we'll see today is pretty much all that was left."

"Was it the fires that made the town die?" she asked.

"The fires certainly didn't help. I'm not a history buff like you so you should know more about this place than I do," he pointed out.

"Surprisingly enough I haven't studied a lot of state history. My focus was really on the Civil War era. I would love to go to the South for an extended period of time and study some of the places that were so significant to the war," she told him.

"Maybe our journey will lead us there," he said, loving the idea of taking her away to a place she was forced to spend more time with him.

"I'm teaching right now, Hunter. There's no way I could get away for a week at a time," she said with disappointment. That helped ease his bruised ego.

"I might just have to sneak into your classroom and watch you lecture one of these days," he told her. She turned to him, her eyes turning to saucers.

"That's not a good idea," she said quickly.

"Why? Are you a bad teacher?" he asked.

"No!" she said with a scowl. "But people pay good money for college. You can't just come in off the street," she said with a bit of a stutter as if she were thinking quick on her feet to make up a suitable excuse.

"I donate to colleges, so maybe I want to see where my money is going," he told her.

"Do you donate to *my* college?" she asked.

"I'll have to check." He handed the money over most of the time and his financial advisor took care of it.

"Well, sit in on another professor's lecture," she told him.

Hunter could rile her up so easily. It wasn't a challenge at all. But even so, he enjoyed it. And now that he'd come up with the idea, he knew he had to go and see her lecture. She looked damned sexy in her professor getup. He couldn't believe he'd ever thought it unflattering. Maybe by the end of this, he'd even get to live out his fantasy and test out the strength of that cluttered desk in her office.

That thought had him thick and hard again. If he kept allowing his mind to travel to places it shouldn't travel, he was going to be damned uncomfortable for a lot of this treasure hunt.

"How many buildings are in Bodie?" she asked as he found parking and turned the vehicle off.

"There are about a hundred, I think. Some small outhouse structures, houses, at least one church, and the giant mill. They closed most of the buildings to keep them and visitors safe. They are sturdy, and not likely to fall over, but there are a lot of exposed nails, unreliable floorboards, broken glass and any number of other safety hazards."

"I bet you could still get us inside one," she said.

"Maybe," he told her. Yes, he was sure he could get her a private tour. Having the money and influence he did allowed him certain privileges. He didn't like to take advantage of it though. But if Becka insisted on it, he just might be willing to bend his own rules.

At that moment was when Hunter realized the power this small woman held over him. He wondered if it was more than sex he wanted from Becka. Was there something about the *actual* woman that called to him in a way most women didn't? That wasn't a very appealing thought. Hunter didn't want to be tied down, didn't want to be responsible for another person, or be accountable to anyone. He loved his life just the way it was.

Hunter walked next to Becka as they made their way through the town. He watched her excitement as they went past buildings and she stopped to look inside the barred doors and windows.

"I can't believe I've been so close to this place and never came here before," she told him.

"Life without adventure is no fun. Anytime you want to try a new place, give me a call," he replied.

She looked at him in a wondering way that made him want to squirm on his feet. He wanted to tell her that they were just empty words — that he was a busy man and once he was gone from this mission, he wouldn't be back. But he couldn't seem to say it.

"Better be careful what you promise, Hunter," she said with a wink that surprised him. Then the moment was broken as they continued on.

They turned a corner, and a rattling sound made Becka jump backward as Hunter caught her. A rattler was two feet away from them and Becka was wearing sandals.

"Be very quiet and back up slowly," he warned her.

He watched the color drain from Becka's face as she stood stiffly at his side without saying a word. He gently nudged her arm, but she still wasn't moving.

"Becka, we have to back away. You've seen rattlers before haven't you?" he questioned.

Finally she turned her head and looked at him, fright in her eyes. If she was this scared of a little snake he wasn't so sure she was going to be able to finish this adventure with him.

The snake rattled again and looked as if it were looking directly at them. Hunter had seen worse things than a rattler, and if he were alone, he wouldn't be frightened at all, but if Becka freaked out on him, he was afraid she was going to get bit.

"I love the desert but sometimes it's a bit more deadly than I like," Becka whispered as the two of them got out of the danger zone.

"Nature can be a real bi—"

"Hunter," Becka interrupted him.

Hunter laughed. He hadn't been corrected in a long time. He found it amusing as he looked down at Becka's professor face. He could imagine her students hanging their heads in shame when she scolded them.

Without a thought, he reached for her, ran his finger down her cheek and cupped her chin, his thumb rubbing against her jaw. Her eyes softened as he got lost in them. The snake Hunter wasn't afraid of. Becka, on the other hand, scared the hell out of him.

He pulled his hand away and took a step back. As much as he wanted this woman, he didn't want to screw it up. The moment had come and gone and as they began moving again, he wasn't sure if he'd made the right decision by pulling away. He just knew that now wasn't the time to get distracted. They were on a mission and if he screwed it up the very first day she would flee faster than a hummingbird.

When they'd completed their objective, maybe he would take a few extra days — or weeks — and finish what he'd started the night before. She was worth sticking around for — at least for a while. He would bed her again. There would be too many regrets if he didn't.

They walked again in silence for several moments and then found the cemetery. Excitement filled Hunter and he was a little frustrated about it. He didn't want to be having a good time on this adventure. He wanted to be mad at his father for making him go. But as they approached the grave of Rosa May, he knelt down and ran his fingers across the hot stone.

"Is this it?" she asked as she knelt next to him.

"I think so," he told her. Then he was still.

"Where do we look?" she asked.

He was almost afraid to search, because if there was nothing, this might all end. But if there was something, then he had to stay. He wasn't sure what he wanted more. Reaching down he moved a few rocks ... and found the next clue.

Chapter Nine

FOR THREE DAYS and three very long nights Rebekah hadn't seen or talked with Hunter. They'd found the next clue, and separated once they'd arrived back home. They'd each taken a copy of the clue and she'd spent every available moment trying to figure it out while she wasn't in her classroom teaching.

She finally had. They were going for a hike on a mountain on an island off the coast of California. It appeared Hunter's father truly did have a sense of humor. She didn't understand any of it, but she did know that she was now invested in this project.

Her fingers twitched on her phone as she ached to call the man. He'd been so close to kissing her again back in that ghost town. And she'd been more than willing to let him. She didn't want to feel that way, and when logic stepped in and her brain was running the way it should, she knew better than to go down that road.

But when she got lost in the beauty of Hunter's incredible green eyes, logic flew right out the window. She desired him — needed him — in a way she hadn't needed anyone in a very long time. Heck, if she were honest, she would admit she'd never wanted anyone the way she desired him. She found herself dialing Aimee instead of Hunter. Her long lost friend answered on the second ring and enthusiastically invited Rebekah to come to her place.

Putting her phone away, she tucked her notes into her bag and jumped into her car. It didn't take her long to find Aimee's place — a perfect two-story in a suburban neighborhood. It was everything Rebekah had once wanted. Maybe she just needed to accept that her life had taken a different path than she'd planned and appreciate the journey she was on.

"I'm so glad you decided to come over. I didn't warn you that my terror child is going to make our visit less-than-peaceful," Aimee said with a laugh.

Rebekah looked down at the angelic face of the little girl clinging to her mother's leg as she gazed up at the stranger entering her house. Acting on instinct Rebekah knelt down and smiled at the child.

"What's your name?" she asked.

"Sandy," the small child answered in a tiny voice. "I'm three," she added, then she moved away from her mom a little, as if she wanted to trust the person looking at her.

"Looks like you keep pretty busy with your restaurant and beautiful daughter," Rebekah said feeling the smallest jolt of jealousy. She'd wanted to establish her career first, then find a great man and settle down, have two brilliant children …

It all seemed so silly to have a life plan. Having everything mapped out didn't necessarily mean she would be happy. Maybe a bit of a mess was more like it.

"I keep busy, but I think you might be more so than me," Aimee said as she led Rebekah into a living room that was clean, but cluttered with toys. It was homey and perfect.

"I think keeping busy is a good thing. It keeps us out of trouble. I guess we've both come a very long way from that summer ten years ago," Rebekah said, trying to put some enthusiasm into her voice. She wanted it to be a positive thing that they had grown up. It was just that growing up wasn't always as fun as people made it seem.

"We can waste time with idle chit-chat, or we can get straight to it," Aimee said with a sly smile that had Rebekah a little worried.

"What do you mean?" she asked as Aimee effortlessly helped Sandy with a toy before turning her attention back to Rebekah.

"You and Hunter back together again after all these years has got to be setting off smoke signals," Aimee told her with a grin.

Rebekah's cheeks heated as she looked over at the young child, who wasn't paying them the least bit of attention.

"Nothing is going on between us. We're searching for buried treasure, that's all," Rebekah told her friend.

"Hmm, why am I finding that difficult to believe?" Aimee said with a laugh. She casually saved a picture frame from being knocked over, but just barely, before she turned her attention back to Rebekah.

"Because you've always been a meddler," Rebekah told her.

"That's *so* not true," Aimee said with a mock gasp.

It was entertaining to watch how easily Aimee carried on a conversation with her while at the same time, keeping such a keen eye on her daughter. The woman had certainly gotten very good at multi-tasking.

"Hunter's dad left him a map to his inheritance. For some odd reason, he listed my name on the document he left behind. Maybe he had a friend who worked at the college or knew a student. I don't know, but it was an adventure I couldn't say no to," Rebekah said.

"Yes, Hunter's father sounded like he was an eccentric man, but he was wiser than people knew. I have a feeling you aren't going to figure it all out until the very end, and then the treasure will be something you couldn't have ever imagined," Aimee told her.

"It's not *my* treasure," Rebekah pointed out.

"If your name was on those documents, it's as much yours as Hunter's," Aimee countered.

"Nope. I'm simply along for the ride." The adventure of it all was everything Rebekah wanted. She didn't need a prize at the end of the game.

"So if you really want nothing out of it, why spend time with Hunter?" Aimee pointed out. Sandy let out a squeal of joy when a puppy came by and licked her on the cheek before going over to his bed and curling up. The scene made Rebekah smile.

"It's not about spending time with him," Rebekah insisted.

"I don't think that's *all* it is."

"I swear the only reason I'm doing this is that I'm invested in it now," Rebekah said. She couldn't look her friend in the eye.

"Would it make any difference at all if I were to share a secret?" Aimee asked.

Rebekah's heart thundered as she looked at Aimee who was grinning broadly.

"Not at all," she said. But she found her throat tight as she waited for Aimee to continue speaking. She couldn't prod her because she didn't want the woman to know that Rebekah really wanted to hear what she had to say.

"I don't think he's ever forgotten you," Aimee finally said.

"Don't go there, Aimee," Rebekah told her, but that tight feeling in her throat was even worse now.

"I know that summer so long ago was supposed to be a carefree one, where you forgot all about him the moment it was over, but I think the two of you connected, and I don't think that connection has ever broken. You fell in love with him — and though it seems impossible, he was just as in love with you. He never forgot about you. Once in a while when he actually comes around, I've seen him looking out at the water, at places the two of you shared a fire on the beach, or swam in the ocean, and there's a lost look in his eyes. Don't you think that's worth exploring?" Aimee asked.

"It's not a risk I'm willing to take," Rebekah told her. She was now twisting her fingers on the hem of her shirt.

"Why?" Aimee asked as she saved the same picture again from getting knocked over. "I know Hunter can be a pain in the ass, and he hasn't had the smallest inkling of settling down in the past ten years. But he's also a wonderful man who donates to abused kids, and schools, and who holds my daughter like she's precious. There's a lot of good in him — enough to risk your heart for."

Rebekah found herself on the verge of tears. She had to push them away quickly. This was a road she'd sworn she wouldn't go down. "I love that you love him, and I'm glad you've been there for each other. But I can't do it. I can't give up what I've achieved and risk it all for a relationship that was never meant to last."

Aimee gave her a measured look before she let out a long-suffering sigh. She checked on her daughter again and smiled.

"Okay, I'll lay off. Tell me what you've been up to," Aimee demanded.

"I got through college and now I'm teaching. I love what I do," Rebekah told her. It was difficult for her to switch topics so quickly. Her mind was still on Hunter, dang it.

"You graduated early, didn't you?"

"Yes, three full years by the time I was done with my doctorate. I got two years done in high school, and then took extra courses while in my undergrad and graduate programs. I spent all my time studying and working for what I'd wanted for as long as I could remember. I didn't have time to dwell on things of the past."

Her life truly was boring, she realized as she rose to her feet and paced the large room. She'd had one summer of freedom and then she'd been locked down in school ever since. She didn't go out, didn't laugh, didn't *live* life. She'd done more living in the last week than she had in the past ten years. There was something truly wrong with that.

"There's nothing wrong with having the best of both worlds," Aimee pointed out. "You can do your job *and* give yourself time to enjoy life."

"I love my job though, so isn't that enjoying life?" Rebekah asked. Why was she defending her life so much when in her own head she knew something was off? Maybe because if she accepted that she wasn't as happy as she was telling her old friend she was, she would fall until she hit rock bottom with a painful thud.

"Are you happy, Becka?" Aimee asked as she looked at her with knowing eyes.

That feeling of tears stung Rebekah's eyes again as she gazed at her friend. She blinked them away. It wasn't a question she was ever asked, and it wasn't something she thought much about. Maybe it was being back in this place where she'd felt such joy, maybe it was just being around Hunter. Whatever it was, it was messing with her head. She couldn't say she was truly happy.

"I love my job," she said instead.

"That's evasive," Aimee pointed out.

"As you well know, life isn't always black and white. There are many colors to each and every day. I'm not unhappy," Rebekah assured her.

"That's true. Do you follow Hunter's career?" And they were back on the man Rebekah didn't want to think about.

"Yes, I have," Rebekah admitted. There was no reason to lie.

"He's incredibly gifted. He captures images that have life in them," Aimee said with a smile before she nodded her head toward the wall.

Rebekah immediately recognized the framed shot. It was a father clinging to his young son as he ran. You could almost see the man's legs in motion. A tornado cloud was halfway to the ground behind them, far too close. Rebekah had looked at the image, her heart pounding when it had been published in a magazine and online. It had gathered a lot of attention and won him some sort of prize. The father had made it to safety. Obviously so had Hunter.

"Yes, he is," Rebekah said in a whisper as her eyes caressed the image on Aimee's wall.

"Don't give up on him," Aimee told her. Rebekah's gaze snapped back to her friend.

"You really don't want to give this up do you?" she replied with a small chuckle.

"I think the two of you were meant to be together. Now you are here with all of this unfinished business. I hope it lasts," Aimee admitted.

"We've grown up and gone down different paths," Rebekah told her.

"No, not necessarily. I still believe in magic, and so do you. You just have to find it within yourself, and you have to chip down that wall you've built." She paused as she looked at Rebekah as if she were trying to decide if she was going to share something important. Rebekah waited. "I wouldn't own the restaurant if it weren't for Hunter. The bank wouldn't give me the loan. He did — interest free."

"What?" Rebekah knew the man had money but she hadn't been aware he had *that* much of it.

"He's a good man, Becka, he really is. I just thought you should know that," Aimee told her.

Rebekah's mind was spinning. She didn't want to look at Hunter as generous and sweet. She wanted to remember him as a good-time man, not the sort of guy you thought about marrying. It wouldn't happen with them anyway. She was a professor and he couldn't last more than a couple weeks at any location. If she opened her heart to this man again, it would get shattered.

Aimee let Rebekah process her thoughts without interruption. Then Sandy stumbled and fell, letting out a scream. Aimee jumped up and grabbed her little girl, who clung to her.

"She didn't really get hurt. It's just past her naptime," Aimee assured her.

"I'll get out of here so you can lay her down," Rebekah said as she stood.

Aimee tried to argue, but there was so much on Rebekah's mind that she needed to escape. She said goodbye and slipped out the door. One more brick on the wall around her heart had been loosened. She feared the whole wall would soon come crumbling down.

Chapter Ten

THE SUN WAS beginning to set as Rebekah walked down the beach she'd spent so much time with Hunter at. Her visit with Aimee had left her with more questions than answers, and she wasn't sure how she felt about the turbulence of her life. Had she made a mistake coming back to the only place she'd ever felt true freedom? She was thinking more and more each day that she had.

If Rebekah didn't think about what she was missing out on, then she didn't dwell on it. But being back in Hunter's world was making that small hole in her heart grow a little bigger each day. She was being immersed back into a world she had willingly left behind.

Since Hunter had walked back into her life she hadn't gone a single day without thoughts of him. Through the years she'd often dreamed about him, but she'd lived her life, had gone days, maybe even weeks without a thought of him. That was over. Now, she was lucky to go a single hour without wanting to close her eyes and get lost in his gaze.

The sea churned next to her, promising a winter storm. She'd never feared bad weather. Living in Southern California, she embraced it. There weren't seasons where she resided, so when a good storm did appear, she rejoiced unlike the many who ran for cover.

That was just one more thing about her that proved she didn't fit in with the rest of her peers, with her community. She knew there was something wrong, knew she needed to get it all figured out, but she also wasn't sure how to do that without uprooting her entire life.

Kicking a large seashell out of her way, Rebekah turned and began heading back up toward the parking lot. That's when she spotted Hunter. He was about a hundred yards away, standing still in a world of his own as he gazed at her.

Rebekah's heart thundered as she told herself to stop, or change directions. She did neither. If anything, her pace picked up the slightest bit as she closed the distance between the two of them.

There was a new look in the man's eyes she couldn't quite interpret. Rebekah wasn't sure what it meant, but she knew she was tired of fighting how she felt, of fighting the desire that simmered through her veins.

Her loose clothing whipped around her body as she neared Hunter. She didn't care. The clothes could fly away and leave her as bare to him as her soul seemed to be. Rebekah only stopped when she was a foot away from him. They both stared without saying a word, though communication wasn't a problem. It was all being said through their eyes.

"I remember how you would always run to this particular shore when storm clouds began forming, while everyone else would head for the hills," Hunter said. His voice was husky and controlled. Rebekah's breathing became even more shallow.

"Yes, it's certainly coming," she said. She wanted to kick herself. What a shallow, foolish thing to say. There was so much she wanted to put into words, so much she wanted to do, but she couldn't allow her tenuous control to be broken. She was afraid of what would happen if she did.

"I think it's because you hold yourself so tightly, you keep every aspect of your life in a neat little box and you never let go. So when you gaze out at a storm, you see yourself in it, in the darkening skies, in the raging water, even in the lightening slashing down from the heavens. You want to let go of it all, but you can't. So you watch it happen from afar. When the storm hits, you can be a part of it."

The more Hunter spoke, the more Rebekah's breathing shallowed. He was so right, but she couldn't tell him that.

"You don't know me as well as you think you do, Hunter," she told him instead. The look he gave her told her without words that he knew she was lying. Her shrug of the shoulders told him she didn't care.

"Why do you even care what I think?" he asked.

She shouldn't care. But she did. He was the one person who'd truly seen her let go of it all. When she'd been in his arms, there'd been no wall up, there'd been no rules, no obligations. With him, she'd been free.

"I *don't* care," she said, tears stinging her eyes.

"Why don't you just say what you want?" he demanded, some of his cool posture disappearing as he reached for her, grabbing her by the arm and pulling her closer to him, their bodies almost brushing.

"I can't!" she shouted. Her deep breathing made her chest brush against his and she was growing more and more lost by the minute. This was all too much. Thunder rumbled in the distance and she smelled the rain in the air. And through all of it, she was frozen on this beach, aching to be pulled into Hunter's embrace.

"You can, Becka. You can let go and allow me to carry you," Hunter said, his voice gentling as he tugged her those final inches, her body perfectly aligned with his, their eyes connected intimately. "Let go," he pleaded.

For a week, she'd been aching, her frustration building as she dreamed of Hunter both in her sleep and during the day. She saw him even when he wasn't there. She wanted him even if she knew it was foolish to feel that way.

"I can't," she said again, her words whipped away by the building wind.

"We let each other go once before. I won't beg you to let me give you what we both want, but I will certainly give you something to think about," he warned.

His eyes darkened as his face lowered. His lips were less than an inch from her own. Was it a promise or a threat? She wasn't sure. She was beyond caring. She needed to taste him again, to relinquish her last bit of control. But she couldn't tell him that. She wanted him to take it, to take the decision from her.

Another clap of thunder exploded, this one so close, it rattled both of them. Neither looked to the sky. They were too absorbed in each other. All she had to do was lean forward and her misery would end.

"All you have to do is admit you want me," he said. His voice was commanding, insistent. She wanted to fall in line with what he wanted — what they both wanted.

Rebekah wanted to tell him to leave her alone. No, she wanted to tell him to take her. She wanted to *want* to tell him to leave her alone. There was a big difference. She opened her mouth to say exactly that, but it's not what came out.

"I need you, Hunter," she whispered. Her reward was a savage gleam in his eyes. She could barely think, so instead she tried to process the emotion flickering through his dark gaze.

His body was solid as steel as he pressed against her. Rain was close, the ocean behind them thrashing as wildly as her heart. A soft moan escaped her lips and was swallowed up by the storm. It all added to the desire she couldn't push away.

Hunter didn't hesitate any longer. He closed that final gap between the two of them and took her mouth in a punishing kiss, his tongue easily sliding past her open lips as he overpowered her in the most delicious way.

There was no more hesitation as Rebekah met his demands with some of her own. Her fingers climbed up his solid shoulders and grasped at his hair as she tugged him closer, demanded what she so desperately needed.

This kiss was nothing like the one a few nights ago. This kiss promised her a night of passion, of wonder, of things she couldn't even begin to dream about. Time had changed both of them, and not in a bad way.

His hands roamed her back until he reached her curved behind and tugged her into him, allowing her to feel the power of his desire. He was so hard, so strong. She wanted to be lost forever in his embrace.

The desire she'd been feeling was now boiling over, and she wiggled against him, unable to get as close as she wanted to be. She needed him inside her, and even then she feared it wouldn't be enough.

No matter how much she'd tried fighting it, Hunter was the one person who allowed her to be free, and she relished in that freedom. She wasn't willing to let it go — not when she was so happy where she was.

When his lips broke away from hers, a whimper escaped. She clutched at his hair, trying to bring him back. When her eyes opened, she gazed at him and her core squeezed tightly.

"I need you, Becka. Come home with me," he said before bending down and kissing her neck. He knew just the place that made her fall apart.

"Yes," she told him. She was willing to follow him to the pits of hell if that's what it would take to ease this suffering she'd self-inflicted for so many years.

They'd been so good together but even back then, she'd known it would end, knew he would go off to see the world while she stayed and did what she'd been raised to do. But for those few short months they'd had together, none of it had mattered. What had mattered was the two of them being together. That's how she felt at this moment.

But as he gazed at her, the remembered pain of him leaving her behind began to filter through her hormone-addled brain. She'd barely survived re-entering the real world. She'd almost given up all of her plans and dreams so she could chase after him.

Now that she was older, and could hesitantly admit her life wasn't as perfect as she wanted it to be, she wondered if this time she'd be able to pick up the pieces. If she fell into his arms and sated the need within her, would it open the gap of her pain to unbearable trauma?

Was Rebekah willing to take the risk?

She shook as she gazed at him. She watched as careful awareness entered his eyes. He knew she was pulling back. He could fight her on it — and win. She knew that too. She almost wanted him to.

"We can't," she said, feeling the need to break into tears. "This was a bad idea, Hunter."

Rage filtered through Hunter's gaze, but he somehow managed to control it. His fingers pressed tightly into her skin as he struggled with whatever it was streaming through him.

"We both know this is right, Becka," he said through clenched teeth. "You want me as much as I do you."

"This is just a chemical reaction," she insisted as she pushed away from him. This time he let her go and emptiness filled her as ragged breaths huffed out of her.

"I didn't take anything from you. I asked. You answered," he reminded her.

There was a clap of thunder at the end of his words, and the promised rain poured down over them, steam coming off of their overheated bodies. The sight made her knees weak. She wanted to run her tongue along the raindrops dripping over his lips. They'd made love in the rain before. It had been exquisite.

"No, you didn't take what I didn't want to give," she admitted.

"But you've changed your mind." It wasn't a question.

"Yes," she whispered.

"You're damning us both," Hunter growled. He reached out and grabbed her wet hand, pulling it against his body so her fingers were pressed against his solid flesh. The rain had molded his clothes to him and she could see and feel his desire. It made her core tighten even more. She squeezed the slightest bit before pulling away from him.

"It's just desire, Hunter. It means nothing. The need can be met by anyone," she said with sadness. He didn't know her, didn't understand her. Not even ten years ago had he understood who she was. Nothing had changed in their time apart. They could sate each other's needs, but she'd become even more broken and empty after.

It wasn't worth it.

"I'm leaving." She turned and took several steps before his words followed her. She didn't stop as he spoke them.

"This *will* happen, Becka. You can't fight it any more than I can. I'll wait. We will finish what has always been inevitable."

The rain poured down, the sea churned and the skies flashed. Rebekah kept walking. She knew he was right — and that was what frightened her the most. She was losing more control with each passing day. And sadly, she wanted to.

Hunter. It had always been Hunter — and it always would be.

Chapter Eleven

*H*UNTER HAD MANAGED to let Becka get away from him, and he'd even succeeded in staying away from her for a full week. He'd put a pause on their treasure hunting. He'd already been back home for the longest stretch since the summer he'd spent with Becka. Everything within him said to run away, to give up this idea of finding some treasure his father felt he needed to earn.

But instead of running away he found himself pulling up to the campus where Becka worked, found himself walking to the building where he knew she'd be giving a lecture, then slipping inside to hide in the back of the classroom as he gazed at the woman who took his breath away.

Becka was standing at the front of the classroom, a smile on her face as she stood at the podium, speaking. Hunter looked around the room and noticed bored expressions on many of the students' faces. How could they be bored with her up there? He noticed one guy focused completely on her before he turned to the guy next to him and made a comment. His friend made a rude gesture, and Hunter was absolutely certain about what they were talking about. Rage filtered through him.

Someone made a comment that stopped Becka's lecture and she looked up, clear irritation in her eyes. Hunter smiled as he sat back. She might appear young and tiny, but she was a force to be reckoned with.

"I know many of you would rather be anywhere but a history class with the holidays quickly approaching, but those not interested in how this country came to be should be ashamed of themselves. History is vital to who we are and I'm attempting to make it as fascinating to all of you as it is to me. That being said, just remember that you are paying good money to be here and keep your negative comments to yourself," Becka said.

Hunter had to admit he wasn't much of a history buff himself. He did enjoy a good movie on epic battles, but he rarely popped open a non-fiction book. He'd rather live in the moment and see current events. But she had a point. Current events wouldn't be what they are without the history that preceded them.

As Becka continued to speak, he was riveted to his seat. He slouched down, not yet ready for her to know he was there. He wanted this unguarded look at the woman he couldn't get out of his head. She was beautiful and talented and so damn smart. The only flaw he could find with her was that she fought her feelings for him.

"We can now continue discussing the Civil War which still has such a hold on us as Americans that mock battles are still being played out. Why do you think it's such a fascinating piece of our history?"

Living out west, this wasn't something Hunter really thought much about, but it did make sense. Every once in a while he would see a Confederate flag fluttering in the wind on the back of a truck, or hear heated debates over who was right or wrong, or for that matter, what had caused it at all. It wasn't something he'd ever put much thought into, but at the same time, would America be where it was had the Civil War never occurred? He wondered how different the present time would be if no battles had been fought.

He sat there for an hour, listening to the smooth tones of Becka's voice, the questions people asked, and noting the way she thought for a moment before answering. She wasn't just spouting off words to appease her class. She seemed excited by the participation, and involved with the students who actively contributed. It was giving Hunter another glimpse into who she was — and into who he was when he was around her.

When she ended the lecture, most students grabbed their books and ran for the doors. A few climbed down the stadium staircase, and she easily and readily answered their questions. Hunter didn't move from his seat. The last of her students ascended the stairs, a couple looking at him in question, but they passed by without a word.

Becka began gathering her books, and only then did he stand. He didn't make a sound, but suddenly she looked up and their eyes connected. He watched as a shudder passed through her and then her face flushed, her body stiffened.

This woman was destroying him piece by piece, making it impossible for him to sleep, to leave, to do anything other than seek her out — even in her safety zone of a campus. The sound of her beautiful voice lingered in the recesses of his mind as he lay awake thinking of her.

It had only been a week since he'd last seen her and yet, it felt like a year. Maybe it was because they had unfinished business. Hunter was confident he would be able to let this woman go. He just wasn't sure when.

Quickly gaining her composure, the look she sent him seemed to say she didn't need him, nor want him, there. She was telling him he was overstepping his boundaries. Hunter didn't care. He'd never been a rule follower. He went where his heart took him and it didn't matter if anyone else had a problem with it.

"Let's have dinner, Becka," he said as he climbed down the steps, drawing nearer to her. It was insane how his body was seemingly pulled to this woman. Even if he'd wanted to leave in that moment, he didn't think he'd be able to.

Hunter refused to analyze that line of thinking.

"No," she told him as he drew much closer than she was obviously comfortable with.

"We're partners. We have to talk," he said. There were many more things he wanted to say to her, but he hesitated. They hadn't ended on the best note when she'd run away from him on the beach after a scorching kiss. He'd wanted so much more.

"I don't think this partnership is going to work out," she told him, refusing to look at him. That irritated him more than anything else. If she were going to dismiss him so easily, the least she could do would be to look him in the eyes.

"I'm not interested in a new partnership, Becka. I only want you," he said, his voice purposely low and soothing. She seemed like a cornered animal and he didn't want to frighten her away.

"This is stupid, Hunter. We've tried to do this together. It hasn't been working out. I've accepted it. Can't you do the same?" she said. Finally, she looked up and the emotion in her eyes told him everything her words weren't saying.

She was fighting him, sure, but she was fighting herself a hell of a lot more. Why? He didn't understand how so many people bottled up how they felt, and lived a life they couldn't stand. Life might seem endless, but he'd watched in first person as timelines were shortened drastically by a natural disaster or even worse, by another's hands. To repress what you actually wanted was a crime in his own mind. Believing enough in yourself to take what you wanted and deserved was a person's right.

"I think you might be afraid of letting go, Becka. You are enjoying yourself and for whatever reason, that scares you. I won't force you to be with me, but I won't turn you away when you admit to what you want," he assured her.

"I'm a professional, Hunter. I assure you I know how to speak my mind. I don't hide," she said. She looked away from him as she finished that sentence. She did hide and she knew it. He decided not to call her on it.

Instead, Hunter walked around to the back of her desk. She leaned into it to try and pull from him, but he closed her in. He wouldn't take what she wasn't willing to give, but he would certainly hold out a piece of candy to tempt her to give in to her hunger.

"Ten years ago we were young and stupid. We both lived for the moment and we had a wonderful time, but now we're grown up and for some reason, we're drawn to each other. Why not explore that? Why not let go? It can't cause any harm," he told her, his mouth only inches from her own.

His body thickened as her eyes trailed down his face and feasted on his lips. She ran her tongue out and swiped it on her bottom lip before biting down on it as if trying not to speak. He could practically feel her heartbeat increase as her breathing deepened. She was as much in a trance as he was.

"What's the matter, Becka? Hungry?" he asked with confidence.

When her hand lifted, her fingers scorched him through the material of his shirt. He wanted to tug her into his arms, but he didn't want to halt the progress they were making. He also didn't want to kiss her into submission. He wanted her to let go and let him love her because she needed it as much as he did.

Instead of grabbing him though, she pushed. Hunter could easily withstand the pressure but he also had to show her he wasn't trying to control her. With reluctance, he took a step back. The surprise in her eyes was his reward.

Picking up her backpack, Becka began to walk. Hunter was at her side in an instant.

"I have a great job, Hunter. I have a good life. I don't need you coming in and messing it all up," she told her, looking straight ahead.

They reached her office without saying another word. When she stepped inside, he followed her, his eyes going directly to her desk. He grew even harder. This day could go one of two ways.

"I have a lot of papers to grade, Hunter." This time her voice came out strong and determined. He loved the professor voice. It only added to his arousal.

"I'm not letting you quit," he said. He locked her door.

A slight panic flickered through her eyes before she got herself under control. She took in a measured breath and he waited to see what she would say next.

"I'm doing what I want — not caving in to your demands," she told him.

"Okay," he simply said. That seemed to take her back. She gazed at him incredulously and waited for the other shoe to drop. "I've always wanted to learn about the Civil War. I need to catch up on my history," he finished.

"What are you talking about?" she asked with wariness.

"If you won't come to me, then I guess I'm going to have to come to you for *every single lecture*. I'll be your shadow."

"Then you'll have to pay tuition," she snapped.

Hunter grinned. Damn it felt good sparring with her. Never before would he have put so much effort into one woman. Becka wasn't just anyone though — she was incredible and well worth the pursuit.

"I'll register tonight," he told her.

Her hands on her hips, she glared at him for several moments before her shoulders drooped. There was excitement in her eyes though. She was enjoying this as much as he was. He was secure enough to admit that.

"If I tell you I'll think about it, will you go away?" she asked.

"Nope. I want commitment," he said, not willing to budge an inch.

After several moments, he saw her lips twitch. She fought it, but she was enjoying herself. It was looking more and more as if this night might go in the direction he'd hoped.

"Fine!" she snapped. "I'll finish the treasure hunt."

Hunter felt as if he'd just won the lottery. He also couldn't stand not touching her any longer.

"Good. Now that business is over with, it's time for pleasure," he said as he stepped closer to her. She backed away from him, until her messy desk stopped her. Her eyes widened as he laid his hands on the desk and boxed her in.

"Any protests, Becka?" he asked as he lightly brushed his lips against hers.

Fire burned in her eyes. Damn, he hoped not …

Chapter Twelve

UNTER'S LIPS GENTLY caressed Rebekah's and slowly she melted against the desk behind her. No matter how many times she told herself this was wrong, she couldn't seem to stop it — didn't want to stop.

"I've had a fantasy since I was a teenager that involved a teacher's desk," Hunter said with a chuckle as he trailed his lips down the side of her neck.

Because Rebekah had savored that same fantasy she couldn't be anything but turned on even more by his words. When she was locked in her office grading papers for hours on end, she'd thought about a savage beast of a man walking through her door and taking her to a whole new world.

And she had the chance to live out that fantasy right then and there. Hunter's lips reached the V of her neck and she felt cool air touch her skin as he undid the top buttons of her blouse, exposing more of her flesh for him to kiss his way down.

"If you want this to stop, you need to tell me," he warned.

She shuddered in his arms as he pulled her close, then began walking them behind her desk. She was barely coherent as he sat down in her large leather chair, pulling her with him so she was straddling his hard thighs.

He gripped her face, taking a moment to look into her eyes. They were glazed over in her undaunted lust for this man she'd always desired. How could she deny them both what they so desperately needed? What would it hurt to give in for once in her life, to be reckless … and happy?

"Becka?" he questioned. His hands were on her hips and she felt the motion of her body as she swayed into him, rubbing her core against his thickness.

"What?" she asked, not even recognizing her own voice.

"Do you want this?" he asked. This time he wasn't kissing her. This time he was waiting for an answer. She nodded. "That's not good enough, Doc. I need the words," he told her.

Becka wasn't sure what she was going to say, but her mouth opened on a sigh. "Yes, Hunter, yes I want this," she said.

His eyes filled with joy and she knew she'd made the smart choice — the only choice. She could have all the regrets she wanted later. But for this moment he was hers, and she was his. They'd done it before. Maybe not in her college office, but they'd done it all over his property. It made sense for the two of them to come together again.

"Thank you," he said before his mouth crushed hers in a far more ardent kiss. He was done with seduction. Now he was going to possess her. Yes! It was exactly what she needed — wanted so desperately.

Hunter parted her lips and easily slipped inside. She reached for his hair and tugged hard, unwilling to let any more space come between them. She wanted their clothing gone, his body atop hers. She wanted him everywhere and she was growing more and more aroused by the second.

Hunter had a masterful kiss, full of passion and promise. It was never enough, and almost too much to take. She was already regretful she hadn't allowed this to happen sooner. It just felt so damn good.

He tugged on the curve of her butt, their bodies surging together. It would be absolutely perfect if their clothes were out of the way. When he ran his fingers beneath her shirt and up the hot skin of her back, she whimpered in approval. Then he pushed her back from him and she wanted to cry out until his hands circled her waist and rose to her breasts.

He slipped beneath her bra and his beautiful fingers squeezed her hard nipples, making her cry out as he captured the sound with his tongue. All of Rebekah's inhibitions left her as she reached between their bodies and spread her fingers across the bulge trying to break free from his pants.

This time it was Hunter who groaned and she who captured the sound as she squeezed him through the denim of his jeans. Breaking away from the kiss, Hunter leaned back and gazed into Rebekah's eyes. The look he gave her made her feel like the most beautiful woman in the universe.

The space between them didn't last long before he was cupping her cheeks, pulling her back to him for another passionate kiss that had her breathing labored. One of his hands wound behind her head, where he tugged at the clip holding her hair back. It cascaded down her back and he ran his fingers through it, tugging her closer still before pulling her head back so he could access the long column of her throat.

Rebekah reached down with shaking fingers and gripped the bottom of Hunter's shirt, but their bodies were too tightly pressed together and she couldn't get any leverage. Thankfully, Hunter leaned back and tugged on the material himself, his shirt flying across her office. He broke their kiss for only a second to perform the act. Then he was devouring her mouth again.

Rebekah let out a sound of pleasure as her fingers traced the hard planes of his chest, noting the differences in his body from ten years before. He'd been just as solid then, but now he was bigger, more confident, and just as sexy.

Rebekah wanted to taste his skin. Wrenching her mouth from his, he reached for her, but it was her turn to trail her mouth down his solid jaw and taste the salt on the skin of his neck. His scent was intoxicating, making her groan as she sucked the place where his pulse was beating out of control.

Moving further down his body, she ran her tongue over his hard nipple, making his breath hitch. She gently bit down on the tasty dark patch of skin and he trembled before her. She moved across his chest to taste the other side. He was delicious.

"Do you like this?" Rebekah asked before her tongue swirled across his nipple.

"I love your touch," he said through clenched teeth.

Rebekah wanted more. She slid her hands down his muscled stomach and reached for his pants. It was difficult to feel everything from her position on his lap. Lust burning through her, she slid onto her knees, leaned forward, and ran her mouth across the scratchy denim covering his pulsing arousal.

"Becka," he said in a guttural tone.

"Mmm," she replied as she began undoing the buttons on his jeans. "You're going to break out of your pants. Let me help with that."

She reached for his buckle and he stopped her. She looked up in question. "I want to touch you," he said.

"Me first," she told him. She had fought this for so long and now she couldn't be stopped if a tornado ripped through the building. She'd gladly kneel in front of him in the eye of the storm. "I need to," she insisted.

With shaking fingers, Rebekah undid his buttons and reached inside the tight denim. She was too impatient to wait for the pants to come down. As she wrapped her fingers around his thick erection, he jimmied the pants down and then he was free, his beautiful, thick steel too big for her hand to hold. The head was soft and wet.

"You are so hard, so hot and velvety," she said with reverence as she slowly moved her hand up and down his beautiful length. He pulsed in her hand as he groaned in sync to the strokes of her fingers. She ran her thumb over the moisture at his tip and watched in fascination.

Rebekah's core was hot and aching as she continued playing with Hunter. Her mouth watered as she made herself wait before tasting him. The anticipation was part of the fun, she assured herself — for both of them.

Hunter moved his hips, sliding himself easily against the palm of her hand. Rebekah couldn't wait any longer. She leaned forward and on his surge upward, she took him deep into her hot mouth. Hunter's pleasure dripped on her tongue as she squeezed him tightly in her fist. Growing even more excited, Rebekah moved quickly up and down his length, loving his taste, his smell, the groans escaping him. She took him as deeply as she could before moving back to gasp in air before doing it again.

Hunter's fingers wound back into her hair and tugged as he pumped himself in and out of her mouth. She braced herself with one hand while gripping him with the other. She could taste him all night and it wouldn't be enough. His sounds of pleasure grew more intense, and she knew she'd have to stop soon or she'd never get what she truly wanted from him.

With a feral growl, Hunter pulled her from him, stopping with her mouth only inches from his hot flesh. She pushed out her tongue but was too far away.

"Give me a second. If you keep sucking me like that, I'll never last," he said, his voice unrecognizable.

Pride filtered through Rebekah. She had pleased him well, as well as she knew he would do for her. Another surge of moisture ran through her core, making her squirm on the floor as she knelt in front of him.

Hunter didn't ask anymore, he took action, lifting her to her feet and devouring her mouth. He wasn't gentle or slow. He crushed his lips against hers as he steered her backward until the small of her back met the sturdy desk behind her.

Lifting her, he sat her on the desk, sliding his body between her thighs. Rebekah reached for her top, but he disposed of it much faster than she would have been able to. She took pride in the way his hungry gaze devoured her barely covered breasts.

"Lean back," he told her in an urgent whisper.

Rebekah did as he told her, lying back on her arms so she could still see the fire burning in his gaze as he looked down at her splayed out on the desk — a feast just for him.

Hunter bent down and ran his tongue along the line of her neck, all the way to the deep cleavage. Reaching behind her, he unclasped her bra, her heavy breasts spilling out into his awaiting hand. He pulled the bra off with his free hand and then held both her aching breasts as he leaned forward and took a nipple into his mouth.

The sound escaping Rebekah's lips was unlike anything she'd heard before. Joy and pleasure flowed through her in the most beautiful way. Arching her back, she reveled in the pleasure as he sucked one nipple then another, his masterful tongue swirling around the sensitive flesh.

Biting down on the nipple, Hunter reached one hand to her thigh and ran his fingers up the exposed flesh, making her quiver. Her arms gave out and she laid down on the desk, completely splayed out for him. Her body was his to do with as he pleased.

His fingers ran up the edge of her panties and she nearly cried when he didn't touch her where she ached the most. He was taking his time and it was killing her. Squirming with need, she shifted her body, trying to get him to touch her where she wanted.

Taking the message, Hunter sucked hard on her nipple as he slid her panties to the side and reached in, stroking her smooth, wet flesh before pushing inside her tight body. When the panties got in the way, he tugged on the material, shredding them before he dove back inside her body, making her twist on the desk before him as she sought sweet release.

"Please, Hunter. It's been so long," she begged. She wanted so much more than his fingers.

He looked up and the wild light in his eyes only fueled her desire. She felt him shift, heard a packet tear, and then finally felt his pulsing flesh at her entrance. She was about to tell him yes again when he surged forward, burying his thick, hard steel deep inside her, taking every last breath from her.

Hunter paused for a moment as they both reveled in the ecstasy of finally being one again. Her body pulsed as her pleasure reached for its peak. Then he began moving, at first slowly, pushing in and pulling out of her tight flesh.

Those aches began to grow closer and their moans rang out together as he picked up speed, pumping faster, harder, deeper with every single thrust into her body.

"Kiss me," she demanded.

Hunter leaned down, holding one leg so he could push even deeper within her, while cradling her head with the other. His mouth connected with hers and he kissed her hard while their bodies pushed together.

Her desk shook with the power of their lovemaking and Rebekah stopped trying to hold back as he continued thrusting. She wanted the sweet relief only he could give her — and she wanted it right now.

Her climax hit with the force of a sledgehammer the buildup had been so great. She cried out and gripped him tightly as she pulsed over and over again, her entire body shaking with relief.

Hunter let out a growl as he let himself go and as her own orgasm trickled off, she felt him pumping inside her. She held him tight while he let everything go and then collapsed on top of her, their hearts beating as one.

Rebekah didn't want to let him go and there was no way she was going to have regrets about what they'd done. But they were on her desk in her office where they could be interrupted at any time. She was sated, but as he rested inside of her, she realized she could do it again and again with him and still never have enough.

Even Knowing that, she also knew they still couldn't work as a couple. They'd proved that ten years earlier.

Rebekah had to cherish this moment and hold on to it, because she wouldn't allow it to continue. Though she was nowhere near ready to let the man go yet, she pushed against him and he leaned back before pulling out of her and reaching down.

She wanted to watch as he removed the condom, but she felt her cheeks heat and she looked away as she stood and reached for her discarded clothing, beginning to put it on.

"You don't have to look away," Hunter told her.

"We need to get dressed," she said, putting a bit of aloofness into her tone.

"Are you already trying to pull away from me?" he asked. By his tone she could tell he was frowning.

"That was wonderful, Hunter. I don't regret a single moment," she said, not really knowing how to answer.

"Yes, it was. We can go back to my place and do it again," he said as he reached around her, his hands clasping over her stomach. She wanted so desperately to lean back against him and accept what he was offering.

She pulled away instead.

"I don't regret what happened," she repeated. "But we have a job to do and I don't want you to now think we're going to be sleeping together while we do it."

Finally she managed to look up at him. She expected to see anger, or resentment on his face, so when he smiled she was thrown for a loop. She waited, afraid to keep speaking. She wasn't sure what would come out of her mouth.

Hunter stepped forward and wrapped his hands around her before bending and taking her lips in a sweet kiss. She instantly fell under his spell and realized he could so easily seduce her again. It would take zero effort on his part.

But before she could sink too far, he pulled back and gave her that same smile, the one that had her heart thumping erratically.

"Good luck in trying to keep your distance from me," he finally said. He took a few steps away. "I won't force you into anything, but if today proved one thing, it's that you want me just as much as I want you. We're magnets to each other and no matter how hard either of us tries to pull away, we're simply drawn back together."

"What does that even mean?" she asked with desperation as he reached for her office door.

He just gave her one more smile and then slipped out her door. Rebekah fell back into her chair and closed her eyes, but that only led to images of the two of them and what they'd just done together. She'd never be able to be in her office again without thinking of Hunter. The scoundrel had known that from the first kiss.

And the wall Rebekah had been trying to keep between the two of them crumbled just a little bit more.

Chapter Thirteen

REBEKAH COULDN'T REMEMBER the last time she'd been on the sea in a boat, enjoying the wind blowing in her hair, the clear skies, and the smell of salt in the air. She wished she wasn't enjoying herself so much, but she couldn't help but love being in the open water, away from the hordes of people who lined the shores.

The waves were calm, and the wind was mild. If it weren't for Rebekah's nerves, which were scattered since she hadn't spoken to Hunter since their lovemaking, she would be in a brilliant mood.

But she wasn't going to think about the fact that she was alone with Hunter, or that they were going to a small island where the chances of seeing another person were basically non-existent.

She was going to be a professional and enjoy her adventure with him — maybe get some of this restlessness out of her system. Hunter wasn't a man who would ever settle down. He was too full of excitement, too ready to seek the next big thrill. That was okay. She accepted that — or at least she was trying to.

Even knowing all of this, Rebekah was exhausted. She hadn't been sleeping well, and it was a good thing they weren't doing rock climbing or anything too strenuous, or she feared she would either slow them down or end up at the bottom of a canyon.

The silence between the two of them had been terrible though, and she was itching to talk about anything just to shut up the screaming in her head. Normally Rebekah was such a smart woman. But when Hunter was involved it seemed she lost at least half of her brain cells.

They arrived at the island after a two-hour boat ride, and both of them slipped into their hiking boots and hats. It was a normal, sunny California day, and they had a map to follow.

"Do you have the food?" Hunter asked.

The sound of his voice after so much silence made her jump. Then she felt foolish and let out a nervous giggle.

"Yes, got it. Let's see how well my legs are going to do on dry land. It's been a long time since I've been on a boat," she said. Her voice cracked a bit. How long had it been since she'd spoken last? It might have been a good six hours. That was odd.

"I have faith in you," Hunter told her. For a moment their eyes met, and there was so much unspoken between them in those few minutes that it took Rebekah's breath away.

She wondered if it was truly possible for a person to change. Was she holding on to the past so she could protect her present and future? The more she was with this man she'd been so in love with, the more she wondered. But that was a dangerous road to go down, and she was torn.

They slowly began walking the path of their map, in search of the next clue on their treasure hunt, and soon the stress of the past few days began to fly away. Although there weren't any other people about on the small island, there was a world of color and sound to keep Rebekah highly entertained.

Soon, stress and anxiety were replaced by magic and possibilities. She could keep dwelling on her possible heartache, or she could live in the moment and enjoy it for what it was. She chose the latter.

The map led them to a set of caves, and Rebekah's heart was racing.

"We're going to need these head lamps," Hunter told her as he pulled them from his pack.

"Are you sure it's safe in there?" she asked.

"I thought you wanted adventure," he pointed out.

"I think it all seems a lot more glamorous in my mind, when I'm sitting behind the safety of my desk," she said with a nervous laugh.

"I won't let anything happen to you," he told her.

She looked over at him and wondered if he truly meant those words. She wanted to question him about it, but she'd decided to go with the magic. In her magical world, she didn't need to ask those types of questions.

They stepped inside the dark caverns and Rebekah stayed close to Hunter as the walls narrowed, some places so tight they had to squeeze through individually. Other spots were large enough for them to walk side by side.

"How big are these caverns?" she asked him. Her voice echoed off the walls in an eerie way that made her nudge a little closer to Hunter. She felt better when she was touching him. It would be so easy to get lost in the cold, dark place.

"I'm not sure," he said. "There's a ledge. Let's sit down, have a snack, and try to figure out this map."

She followed him to the ledge and pulled out their sandwiches while he studied the map before him. The two absentmindedly scanned the map, then shined their lights around the cavern.

"We go to the left here, through that tunnel, then it shouldn't be more than another half mile," he said as they finished their food.

"You're sure we aren't going to get lost in here, our bones found in a hundred years?" she questioned as she zipped her pack up and stood.

"I can't guarantee anything," he said with a chuckle. "But if we do get lost forever, at least we're together."

"That's not reassuring," she told him. "Maybe we should just head back." They were already deep into the mountain. She wasn't sure how much farther she wanted to go.

"Then our treasure hunt will be over. We won't know where the next clue will lead us," he told her.

"I never have been one to give up," she said with a sigh.

"When this is all over and I figure out what it was that my father wanted me to learn, the two of us will celebrate in a beautiful place with an expensive bottle of champagne," he told her.

"It doesn't have to be expensive," she said as they made their way down the narrowing tunnel.

"What?" He seemed confused.

"Some of the best things in life cost nothing," she said.

He stopped and turned toward her. It was dark all around them, but the lights attached to their heads were bright, and she wondered what he was trying to find in her expression. She wasn't good at masking how she felt.

"I agree with that. I've been all over the world and I've run from this place so fast and so hard that it gave me whiplash, but if I'm being honest with myself and with you, I haven't felt this happy in a long time. Maybe what I've been seeking all along has actually been here."

It was the most serious thing Rebekah could ever remember Hunter saying. She should respond, should lift her hand and caress his cheek, should ask him to expand on what he was saying. But she chickened out, and the moment was lost. He turned and began walking again.

They were mutually silent as they moved farther along the path until it opened up into another cavern.

"I thought I heard running water," Hunter told her.

They walked carefully forward and found an underground stream. Rebekah leaned down and felt the water. It was ice-cold and she would bet it tasted exceptional. She wasn't going to test her theory out though. There were too many fears of what could be in it.

"We're in the right place," Hunter said as he pulled out the map and showed it to her. "Look for the rock cropping."

The two of them circled the large cavern until they found the shape on the map, a pile of rocks. They dug into it and found a box.

"I can't believe it's here," Rebekah said with excitement as she held the box in her hands. "Is this the treasure?"

Hunter looked at the small item. "I doubt it," he said. "If so, my inheritance is awfully small."

"It's not about what the item is, it's about the journey," she told him. "How can you not be excited about this?"

"Maybe because I'm irritated with my old man," he said. There was something in his tone that told her it was so much more than that.

"I think it's more likely that you miss him," she said quietly as she handed him the small wooden box.

Hunter was silent for several moments. "Maybe I do. Maybe I could have made a few different choices in my life," he admitted.

That was more progress than Rebekah could have ever hoped for.

"Open it please before I die of anticipation," she said, unable to contain her excitement.

Hunter lifted the lid and they both gazed inside. There were only two words — "Algoma Resort" — and an envelope with another map.

"What is this?" she asked.

"Looks like my dad wants me to go see my brother Luke," he said with a sigh.

"So the hunt is still on?" She couldn't believe how grateful she was to hear that.

"The hunt is still on," he told her with a chuckle. "We might as well get out of here. By the time we get back to the mainland, I'll be ready to chew off a leg."

"I have granola bars," she said, taking off her pack and pulling out a couple.

Hunter accepted one and with their newest piece of treasure tucked into his pack, they began to make their way back out of the tunnels. He was strangely quiet as they made the two-hour trek out of the mountain. When they finally saw light again, it was later than they'd realized.

The sun was low in the sky and they would be hard pressed to make it back to shore before dark. Rebekah didn't mind a sunset boat ride with Hunter at the helm. Her emotions were already messed up. What would a bit more confusion hurt?

They began the path back down to the boat, and that's where things went severely wrong. Rebekah heard the rattling too late. Hunter was several feet away from her and she turned in time to see the snake's head coming toward her. She stumbled back, but not far enough.

The thing struck her fast, latching onto her leg, where immediate pain made her scream before she fell backward. Hunter caught her before she hit the ground. He kicked the snake and it went flying off into the woods.

"I'm right here, Becka," he told her as he cradled her in his arms, and then began running down the trail to their boat.

It didn't take them long to get there, but her leg was on fire. He climbed aboard their boat and laid her down on the deck. He didn't hesitate a single second before he ripped the bottom of her pants to see the area better.

"I need to grab the first aid kit. I'll be right back," he told her.

Rebekah couldn't fight tears from falling down her face. She'd never been bitten before and she was grateful for that. The pain was excruciating. She reached down to rub the spot, but Hunter was back and pushed her hand away.

"Don't touch it. I need to clean the area and then we have to get you medical help," he said. The panic in his voice wasn't reassuring her. "I should have been faster," he told her as he washed the area, tying a dressing a few inches above the bite mark.

"It's not your fault," she told him, her teeth beginning to chatter.

Shooting pain radiated from her leg. Her head was growing light and fuzzy, and her heart raced. She began to twist as he did the best he could with the supplies they had.

"You have to try to keep still," he said. His voice was calm, but with an edge that told her she wasn't doing well.

"I'm trying," she said. Dizziness was overtaking her and Rebekah wasn't sure if she was going to remain conscious for much longer. She didn't care. At this point, passing out would be a relief.

"I'm going to get you help." Hunter leaned down and gently kissed her lips before he was on his feet again. Rebekah felt the motion of the boat as he reversed out of their place and then floored it, in a much bigger hurry to get back than he'd been to arrive at the island.

Rebekah gave into the dizziness and let the darkness pull her under.

Chapter Fourteen

RIFTING IN AND out of consciousness, Rebekah preferred the blackness because each time she was awake, she felt the burning throb she didn't want to feel. Who would have guessed that two small puncture wounds could send pain throughout the entire body?

Her time in the hospital had been a blur, she'd been so out of it. She barely remembered Hunter bringing her to his place and lying her down. But as she blinked her eyes open and tried to focus on the slowly spinning ceiling fan, she felt the dull throb in her leg and knew it was time to wake up, if only for a dose of pain meds.

A sound escaped her throat and made her jump before she realized it was her making the noise. Even so, panic invaded her until she felt the soft touch of fingers against her cheek.

"You're okay, Becka, I'm here with you," Hunter whispered.

Turning her head, she found him lying next to her. Her heart slowed its erratic rhythm as she focused on the man who had been so quick to respond during her emergency. She was grateful he'd been there.

"Hunter." Her voice cracked as she spoke his name. She closed her mouth and tried to clear her throat. She was unbelievably thirsty, but she wasn't sure she could get the words out. It was awful how weak she felt.

Without her asking, he sat up and slowly lifted her into a sitting position before he grabbed a glass of ice water with a straw.

"Take a drink. I'll get your meds," he told her.

Her fingers trembled as she took the glass from him. He didn't let go until he was sure she wasn't going to drop it. When he left to get her meds, she felt a moment of panic. It was ridiculous. She'd been on her own for a very long time and even being sick, or damaged as was the case, she didn't want to lean on anyone — knowing it was safest to count on herself.

"What happened?" she asked, trying to recall everything after the snakebite.

"I got you to the hospital and your leg was severely swollen. They gave you the medicine and kept you overnight. I brought you home this morning. They said to give you the pain meds and to keep you warm and watch out for you. The swelling already went down and you responded great to the treatment."

"Good. I hate hospitals," she told him.

"I remember," he said with a chuckle. "I'm not a big fan of them either."

"We have to go to the next clue," she said. Her voice was coming back and she was afraid he was going to finish the treasure hunt without her now that she'd been injured.

Hunter chuckled again. "It's not going anywhere. The doctor insisted on at least a few days of rest. We'll reevaluate then," he told her.

"You can't do it without me," she said.

"I wouldn't dream of it," he assured her.

That helped her relax. She didn't understand why this journey was so important to her, but if it were to come to the end without her there, then it would all have been for nothing. Maybe she was so worried about it because she'd never gotten closure with Hunter before, when as a teen, she'd been so in love with him. Maybe this was the closure she needed to finally move on with her life.

"Where are we?" she asked as she looked around at the unfamiliar bedroom.

"We're at my brother's property, in a guest house," he said.

"Oh." She wasn't sure how she felt about that. "In the cabin?"

"No, that's a bit too rustic. We're in one of the guest houses. It's not luxurious, but I sort of like it."

"Me too," she told him. And she did. She felt at home and completely comfortable — maybe too comfortable if she were honest.

"I feel so funny," she said. Her head was foggy and she was so dang tired, though the sun was coming in through the curtains and it was obviously the middle of the day.

"The meds will make you a bit fuzzy, but without them you would be in a lot of pain," he told her as he gave her more pills. She took them without hesitating.

"My stomach is a bit sore, too," she said, not liking the uncomfortable feeling.

"Let me get you some food."

He began to leave and she felt that stirring of panic again. "I don't think I could eat," she said before he was able to step from the room.

"Let's just get some soup and bread into you. Then you can rest more."

"Do you have to leave?" Why was she so scared about that?

"I'm not going anywhere, Becka," he assured her. He leaned down and gently kissed her lips before he stood and walked from the room.

She knew she shouldn't get too comfortable, but she couldn't help it. Normally when she was sick, she was alone in her small apartment, suffering in silence. She had pulled away from everyone in her life, living too much like a hermit. Maybe it was time to stop that when this adventure was done. It was too easy to grow depressed while watching the world go by instead of actively participating. She didn't want to wake up one day and regret every decision she'd ever made.

She heard Hunter rattling around in the kitchen and she leaned back against her pillows and closed her eyes, enjoying the sound of another person being in the house with her. It was something she could most certainly get used to. That was a frightening thought, but she didn't care. The meds were doing their job and she felt free and uninhibited.

When he returned, the smell of the soup should have awoken her appetite, but as he placed a tray in her lap, she still couldn't muster up a desire for food. She looked down at it in disinterest.

"I know it's hard to eat, but I want you to make an effort," he told her.

He carefully sat down on the bed next to her and leaned back on his own pillows as he looked pointedly at her food and then her face. She didn't want to seem ungrateful for the effort he'd put into making her something.

"Thank you," she told him.

"I find that I like taking care of you," he said. He reached over and plucked a piece of fruit off her tray and munched on it. A bit of juice escaped his mouth and he caught it with his tongue. Even in her drug-induced stupor, she felt a stirring within her at the sight.

She certainly had a problem if she was on her sickbed and the only appetite she could muster was for the man next to her. So she wouldn't give herself away, she quickly picked up her spoon, taking a tentative bite of the soup. She could barely taste it, but at least it didn't upset her stomach. With much effort she forced herself to take small sips in between bites of the crusty bread.

"You know, you scared the hell out of me," Hunter told her after a few moments.

"How so?" she asked. She finally pushed the food away. She'd eaten at least half.

"I don't like seeing you hurt," he said.

"We all get hurt," she pointed out.

"Can you eat a bit more?" he asked.

"No. I'm stuffed," she said. He sighed but he took the tray away from her and set it on a table in the room before joining her on the bed again. This time when he sat, he pulled her against him so she was now leaning on him.

Though he was much harder than the pillows, he was also warm and comforting and she cuddled into him, feeling sleepy and taken care of. His fingers reached into her hair and she allowed herself to relax against him as he caressed her head.

"I will make sure nothing like that ever happens to you again," he said. His voice was coming to her through what sounded like a tunnel. It was oddly nice.

"You're Mr. Adventure. You put yourself at risk all the time," she pointed out.

"That's me," he said, his voice confident. It made her smile.

"So it's okay for you to scare the people who love you, but it's not okay for me to go on an adventure and take a risk?" she asked.

"Taking a risk is one thing, but getting an injury that could permanently affect you is another."

"It's not like I sought out the snake and told it to come and bite me," she said with a small chuckle. She was too warm and comfortable to argue very effectively with the man.

"No, but you have to be more careful. You were tired all day. Maybe if you were getting more sleep you'd be more focused."

"It was a snake, Hunter. There's nothing I could have done about it. One second I was walking and the next it was just there. But I promise you I'll be as careful as possible."

"I know I'm being ridiculous. It's just that you really scared me," he confessed.

"I like that you've been worried about me," she told him. She snuggled in a bit closer to him and felt all her pain and worry drift away. It might be the medicine she'd taken, or it might be his fingers rubbing her head. Whatever it was, it was the magic formula and she wasn't in a hurry to move.

"Let's get you laid down," he said as he began to pull her away from him.

"No," she said, an edge of panic in her voice.

"What? Are you in pain?" he asked, stopping his movement immediately.

"No. I just don't want to move," she said.

Hunter sighed as he squeezed her gently.

"Then we won't," he told her. She felt his lips against her temple and she closed her eyes.

This time when the fogginess took her under, she didn't care. She was safe in Hunter's arms and she knew he wasn't going to leave her — at least not while she was injured. She was almost grateful for that dang snake now.

Rebekah fell asleep with a content smile on her lips.

Chapter Fifteen

I T WAS PITCH black out when Hunter was awoken by Rebekah stirring against him. His body throbbed where her leg pressed against his groin. She was wrapped completely around him, which was something he'd normally love, but at the moment, with her being injured, he wasn't a huge fan of the situation.

He wanted to kick himself for having such an insensitive response to the woman when it hadn't even been forty-eight hours since she'd been hurt. Man, had he been terrified when he'd seen that snake strike and watched the pain filter across her face before she'd let out the anguished cry.

His heart had raced and his mind had completely blanked for a few seconds before he'd managed to prod himself into action. He had to help her — save her. He had to make sure nothing happened to her.

Hunter had been a fool for a long time. He knew this beyond a doubt. He'd always sought adventure, the more dangerous the better, and he hadn't allowed himself to stay in any place long enough for roots to grow. Only now, he didn't exactly understand why that was.

As he'd fallen asleep with Becka in his arms, he'd felt more peace than he ever had while doing all those things he'd thought he needed to do to be happy. What if all he'd needed all along was this one woman? He didn't even want to think about that, because if it were true, he'd already wasted too much time.

He shifted and Becka moaned, instantly making him feel guilty.

"Did I wake you?" he asked, pulling her closer to him, though it caused him almost unbearable pain.

"No, I feel like I've been sleeping for a million years," she told him. She snuggled in closer, instead of pulling away, and Hunter couldn't help but like it. The only light shining in the room came from the hallway, but it was enough for him to be able to see her features.

"You've been in and out for almost forty-eight hours, so I can see how that would feel like a million years," he told her with a laugh.

"Are you serious?" she gasped. She pulled back to look at him with horror in her eyes.

"You were obviously tired and needed the rest. Do you need more pain meds?" he asked.

She shook her head against him. "It aches a little, but if I take them, then I'm just going to fall asleep again and I don't want to do that," she insisted.

He looked over at the clock and saw it was three in the morning. That meant he'd been sleeping for the past nine hours straight. He couldn't remember the last time he'd slept that long. He'd been up for about thirty-six hours before that, but still …

"Why don't I go and draw a bath for you? I'm sure it will feel like heaven," he suggested.

The thought of her in a soapy tub had his body growing even more thick and hard. This caretaking was surely going to kill him. But it would be worth it when she was at a hundred percent. Then he could go back to seducing her again.

"That actually sound perfect," she said. "But I can do it myself."

"Nope. Doctor's orders are that you rest and be served," he said. He found himself reluctant to untangle their bodies and he would swear she whimpered when he pulled away from her. That made his lips turn up as he practically hummed on his way to the bathroom.

Hunter took a two-minute shower to wash away the rest of his sleepiness, then started the bath for Becka. He was grateful when he found some fruity sudsy stuff beneath the counter. He knew for sure his brother hadn't put that in there, so it had to be his wife who'd thought of it.

When the tub was full he came back into the room and found Becka sitting on the edge of the bed. She seemed exhausted from doing even that much. He walked over and she looked at him with frustration.

"I can't believe how tired I am, especially considering how much I've been sleeping," she told him.

"It's understandable. I'm sure the bath will help," he assured her.

She tried to push up and he put out a hand stopping her. She looked at him in confusion and he smiled. He really was enjoying being the one in charge and being her knight in shining armor. He'd never played the role before.

Without asking for permission, he reached down and scooped her into his arms. A gasp escaped her, but her arms automatically circled his neck to keep her from wobbling as he swiftly moved to the bathroom.

"I could easily walk," she said.

"I know," he told her. He didn't set her down until they were at the tub. "I'll be glad to help you get out of your pajamas." Heat ran through him at the thought, even though he'd only said it to tease her.

Unbelievably, Becka's cheeks flushed. It wasn't as if he hadn't seen her naked before. But maybe one of the qualities that attracted him to her was her innocence. He'd always thought he liked bad girls, but none of them compared to his sweet Becka. Damn, was he getting some girly thoughts in his head. He needed a shot of whiskey, STAT.

"I'm good now. Go away," she told him as she pushed against him.

"I'm leaving the bathroom door open," he said.

"No!" Her voice was loud as she practically shouted. "I want privacy."

"I'll leave it cracked and I'm coming back in exactly ten minutes to check on you to make sure you haven't drowned," he said. He didn't give her a chance to argue that time. He left, leaving the door cracked. He did go to the kitchen so she'd have privacy to do whatever she had to do before slipping into the tub.

Ten minutes drug by as he fixed himself that shot of whiskey and grabbed a donut from the cupboard. It was an odd combination, but there was nothing normal about his current situation, so it was a fitting midnight snack.

When the clock told him ten minutes had passed, he moved quickly to the bathroom and tapped on the door. "You awake, Becka?" he asked quietly.

"Yes," she said with a relaxed sigh.

"I'm coming in," he told her.

He stepped through the doors and wondered if a healthy, thirty-three-year-old man could have a heart attack. The sight of her beneath the suds made sweat break out on his skin. Maybe checking on her hadn't been his best idea ever. How could he have sex on the brain when the woman was injured? He was a monster, he decided.

"Hunter," she said on a sigh that had his erection throbbing painfully.

"Yes," he responded, the word a bit too terse.

"Thank you for taking such good care of me. You didn't have to do all of this," she said. She wasn't looking at him. Her head was leaned back against the tub, her eyes closed.

"I've enjoyed it," he responded. Then he felt himself moving forward instead of away. He should leave, come check on her again in another ten minutes, but he couldn't pull himself from the room.

"It still means a lot to me," she told him.

"What kind of man would I be if I left you in your condition?" he said. He found himself sitting on the edge of the tub, his fingers reaching into the water. He didn't touch her, but it was killing him not to.

"It wasn't your responsibility," she said. "Now just accept the thanks." She chuckled as she stirred. Hunter was mesmerized by a place in the middle of the tub where the bubbles had separated.

He could see a piece of her smooth creamy skin below the surface of the water and without thinking he reached for her and ran a finger over her stomach. Her eyes flew open and their gazes connected. He was sure there was enough heat between them to make the water boil.

"Want to join me? The water is nice," she said, her voice sounding shy all of a sudden.

Hunter knew he should say no. He knew a gentleman would walk away and make sure she was at full health and not take advantage of the situation. But he found himself standing and reaching for his clothes as he began to shed them.

Becka didn't look away from him as he pulled off first his shirt and then slipped his pants down. He was throbbing as he stood there beside the tub. Nothing could hide his desire for this woman. She looked down and his body pulsed as if she'd caressed him with her fingers instead of her eyes.

Carefully he stepped over the edge of the tub and she leaned forward. Hunter sat behind her, then circled his arms around her and tugged her against him. His heart thumped against her back and he suddenly felt a deep sense of calm at having her in his arms again. This woman was changing him in so many ways, and he didn't care.

Though desire was certainly on his mind, he also felt perfectly content to simply hold her while she got feeling better. When she did, he was certain he wanted to have another bath with her — that was for sure, one that gave them both an incredibly happy ending.

They sat in the tub as he gently caressed her, the water cooling off. Hunter couldn't honestly remember feeling more at peace than he did in this very moment. Becka turned her head so she was resting it against his neck.

"I'm incredibly tired still. I don't know how it's possible after all the sleep I've had but ..." Becka trailed off as she leaned against him. He felt the whisper of her lips against his neck and a pleasant tiredness fell over him as well.

Keeping her in his arms, he stood and pulled them both from the tub. He took his time drying Becka off as she swayed on her feet. Touching her, even with the towel between her body and his fingers, had him hard and ready to take her, but he mentally yelled at himself to calm down. This night was about her, not him.

He dried himself quickly, then wrapped the towel around his hips before he lifted her into his arms again, her naked body pressed against his chest. He set her on the bed and she went to lie down and he stopped her.

"Let me get you a dose of medicine," he said.

"Okay," she replied, her eyes droopy, her face relaxed.

He hurried and grabbed medicine and then helped her lie down. Then he threw on some sweats before he climbed in behind her and tugged her into his arms. Desire was still with him, but it was pushed to the back of his mind as his hand splayed out on her stomach and his body cradled hers.

Finally, Becka was letting down her guard. Hunter was getting a glimpse of what it could be like between the two of them forever. He wasn't sure he would let her retreat again. Not after what she'd shown him — not after getting what he hadn't even known he wanted.

Home. Hunter felt as if he was finally home he realized before sleep pulled him under.

Chapter Sixteen

TRETCHING, REBEKAH CAME up with cold sheets when she awoke and reached for Hunter. Emptiness filled her as she opened her eyes and looked for the man who'd been with her for the past three days.

She turned on her back and looked up at the ceiling as the fan slowly turned in circles. Her body ached in more ways than one, but the pain was more manageable this morning. Her heartbreak seemed a far worse condition at the moment.

She'd let herself go and enjoyed being in Hunter's arms, in relying on him. But as she faced the reality of a new day without him, she wondered if she'd made a monumental mistake. She'd slipped and that wall around her heart had come crumbling down. She wasn't sure she'd be able to build it back up again this time.

Panic invaded her when she started to think about what had happened during the past few days. Had it all been nothing more than a dream? That thought didn't sit well with her. Their time together had been so beautiful; there was no way it could all be in her head.

"You slept well. I'm glad to see you awake."

Rebekah jumped at the sound of Hunter's voice. She turned to find him walking into the room, a tray balanced on his hand and a lazy smile resting on his lips. It was the most beautiful sight she'd ever seen. Yep, that wall was certainly down, and she had no desire to rebuild it.

He helped her sit up, and she quickly grabbed the blankets, realizing she was naked. He smiled knowingly, as if able to read her mind, and placed the tray on her lap. It had eggs, toast, and coffee, and the smells were heavenly. Rebekah's stomach growled. She hadn't eaten much in days and now that her body wasn't in excruciating pain, it wanted to be fed.

"Thank you for this," she told him.

He moved over to the window and opened the curtains, the bright morning light almost too much for her eyes. But then he opened the pane and fresh air blew in and she was in heaven. Rebekah wouldn't mind waking up like this each and every day.

"I have found it's been a pleasure taking care of you while you're weak and pathetic," he said as he sat down in a chair beside the bed and sipped his coffee.

Her fork pausing halfway to her mouth, Rebekah glared at the man. "I am certainly *not* pathetic," she told him.

Hunter chuckled as he smiled at her. "Okay, I'll take that back. You aren't pathetic, but you have been weak and adorable," he said.

"I feel weak. I'm not used to it," she grumbled.

"Eat all your food and you'll begin to get some of your energy back," he assured her.

She put some of her scrambled eggs on a piece of toast and lifted it to take a bite. It was utter perfection. "This is good," she told him when her mouth wasn't full.

"I make a few things well," he said. It was almost odd to see him so relaxed, leaning back in his chair as if he had nothing better to do than sit there visiting with her. "How did you sleep the rest of the night?" he asked.

"I slept well," she mumbled before diving back into her food.

"Good. I don't want to see you retreating again," he said. Something in his tone alerted her and she looked up. He gazed at her, his eyes intense. Maybe he wasn't as relaxed as she'd thought.

"I don't retreat," she told him.

She finished her food, wishing she'd gone more slowly so she had something to focus on besides Hunter.

"Do you need more medicine?" he asked, and she was thankful for the change of subject.

"I don't think so," she told him. "I'd like to do something other than stay in this bed all day and if I take more pills, it'll knock me out again."

His eyes changed as his gaze skimmed her body. Even beneath the protection of the blankets she felt as if he was seeing every inch of her. That left her far too vulnerable.

"I can think of worse places to spend a day than in a bed," he said as he winked at her.

He rose and her heart raced as he stepped forward. He leaned down and kissed her lips just long enough to have her melting against the pillows propping her up. This man was so damn dangerous — and she loved every second of it.

The kiss ended too soon. He grabbed the tray and began to walk from the room.

"Where are you going?" She hated how rattled she felt when he left. She blamed her injury and the medication that was surely still coursing through her system.

"I'm going to clean up our breakfast dishes. Why don't you take a quick shower and then join me in the living room for a while? I'm sure it'll feel good to move around a little bit," he told her.

He stood in the doorway and waited while she clutched her blankets to her chest. "That sounds perfect. I'll come out in a little while."

He stood there like he had all day. She sent him a look that spoke volumes and finally he chuckled and walked away. She didn't know why she didn't want to stand up naked in front of him. It wasn't as if there was anything he hadn't seen before. Maybe it was because it made her feel vulnerable and she was already too indebted to him to feel any other weak emotion.

Whatever it was, she waited a few more seconds to be sure he wasn't coming back, then she hopped from bed and moved as quickly as she could across the room to the bathroom. She only limped a little. Her leg was sore, as was the rest of her body, but it wasn't unbearable anymore.

Rebekah's shower sapped her energy, and she struggled just to dry off. Her pain grew and she fought against it. She didn't want to take more pills and feel groggy, but she wasn't sure if her pride was going to cause her unbearable pain later.

She sat down on the edge of the tub with the towel wrapped around her, trying to talk herself into walking back into the bedroom. There was a tapping on the bathroom door a second before it cracked open.

"How are you doing in there?" Hunter asked.

"I'm fine," she told him, but her voice came out weak.

He pushed the door open and walked inside. "You're hurting, aren't you?" he said as he kneeled in front of her and placed his hand on her forehead. "And you're a bit warm."

"I want to go to the living room," she said, on the verge of tears.

"I'll make a deal with you," he said with a smile as he leaned in and gently kissed her. "You can come to the living room where I'll set you up with a nice warm blanket and a book, but you have to take your pills."

Rebekah wanted to fight him, wanted to tell him she was an adult who could make her own decisions, but the longer she sat on the edge of the tub feeling wobbly and weak, the harder it was getting to argue.

"Okay, deal," she finally said.

Hunter smiled at her and she felt as if she'd just won the dang lottery. She was in serious trouble if simply pleasing him made her so happy.

"Good." He picked her up and she didn't fight him. When he walked back into the room, she saw he'd made the bed and set out fresh pajamas for her. As much as she wanted to wear real clothes, she had a feeling she'd be asleep again soon enough anyway, so the pajamas would definitely be the way to go.

Hunter set her on the bed and before she could do anything he slipped her nightgown over her head. Rebekah should insist on taking over, but the more he stepped in and took care of everything for her, the more she wanted to let him.

When he was done helping her dress, he lifted her again and carried her to the living room where he already had a place ready for her.

"I can do basic things," she said with a sigh as she sank down into the couch, her legs propped up on a pillow.

He placed a blanket over her and handed her a book. "I know you can, but I don't ever get to do this. Let me enjoy myself," he said.

He went and grabbed a glass of water and her pills. Rebekah took them and leaned back.

"What will I do when you're gone then?" she asked, hating the vulnerability in her voice.

"Who says I'm going anywhere?" he asked.

Rebekah's heart raced at his words and she wanted to ask him what he meant by that, but the moment passed and she was too scared to push it. Her pills kicked in far sooner than she'd hoped. Before closing her eyes and giving in to the sleep she needed to heal, Rebekah gazed at Hunter at the other end of the couch, staring at his computer.

This domestic scene was something she could get used to. Maybe she'd just freeze the moment for the many lonely nights she was sure were coming.

Chapter Seventeen

HUNTER WAS RESTLESS as he climbed the hill to his brother's place. He felt tense leaving Rebekah for any length of time, but he knew she would be knocked out for hours. Those pills were strong. Maybe she would be well enough by tomorrow to take something a little less potent.

He hoped so. As much as he loved seeing the woman in bed, he didn't enjoy seeing her hurt and helpless. He did like taking care of her — a little too much, if he were being honest.

Hunter didn't even know what in the hell was happening to him anymore. He was sure he wouldn't find any answer with Gabe, but he was the only person around right now, so he sought him out.

Hunter found Gabe on the back deck. His brother looked distracted when he first looked up but that was nothing new. Gabe always had been a workaholic.

"You've risen from the guest house," Gabe said with a knowing look.

"It's not like that. Becka's been sick," Hunter said with a scowl as he sat down beside Gabe.

"And you've been domesticated it seems," Gabe said. "I remember you giving me a lot of shit, so payback's a bitch."

"We're just doing this treasure hunt together — and maybe satisfying some mutual needs. There's nothing more to it than that," Hunter said. But he was confused. He'd come to speak to his brother, so he didn't understand why he was holding back now. Gabe had changed since meeting and marrying Josephine, had changed in really good ways. Or bad ways, depending on how a person were to look at it.

"I don't think so, Hunter. I think you were a fool to leave the girl ten years ago and I think you're fighting a losing battle now," Gabe told him.

Hunter was shocked by his brother's words. For a moment he really didn't know what to say. This wasn't the typical kind of conversation the two of them had shared before. It was throwing Hunter off.

"What happened to you?" Hunter asked.

Gabe chuckled. "I found the girl I can't live without," he told him.

"So does that mean you think all your siblings should settle down?" Hunter grumbled. "Just because you and Luke are all happy and crap doesn't mean the rest of us should fall in line."

"No. I would never claim to be a matchmaker. I'm just saying that I've seen you and Becka together and I think you're made for each other. I've seen you without her and you're reckless and foolish most of the time. Maybe it's true that we need our other half to be whole."

"Whoa, that is just far too much yoga talk for me," Hunter told Gabe. "I'm getting a beer."

"It's only two in the afternoon," Gabe pointed out.

"Well, I've traveled all over the country so it's certainly five o'clock in other places."

Gabe laughed. "Then you might as well grab one for me too, since Josie is gone for the afternoon and I already miss her," he called out as Hunter entered the house. It didn't take him long to get back to his brother, who was giving him a smug look.

"Have you talked to any of our siblings lately?" Hunter asked. He could get used to sitting in one place for a while. That thought should be terrifying, but he'd missed Gabe. Heck, he was beginning to miss all his siblings. He was wanting to be around a lot more.

"Yeah, we've been talking quite a bit more since the old man passed. I don't know if it made us face our own mortality or what, but I do have to say, it feels good to be home again."

"I was thinking the same thing. I was also thinking, I'm not sure I like this train of thought," Hunter mumbled.

"There's something on your mind," Gabe told him. "Are you going to spit it out or do I have to drag it from you?"

Gabe set his computer aside and focused all his attention on Hunter. He had wanted to talk to his brother, but now that the moment was actually there, he wasn't sure what he wanted to say.

"I do enjoy being with Becka," Hunter finally admitted.

Gabe laughed and Hunter clenched his teeth. No wonder men didn't do these sorts of talks the way women did. He'd be surprised if they got through it without fists flying.

"You are making my heart race with your poetic words," Gabe finally said when the chuckles died down.

"And you're making me want to hit you over the head with a beer bottle," Hunter said.

"Not like that hasn't happened once or twice before," Gabe told him. "You always were a magnet for trouble."

"Maybe the adventure alone isn't enough anymore," Hunter said, finally voicing the truth of the matter.

"I don't think you would ever be happy without adventure. I think you might just want a partner to do it with now," Gabe told him, his voice serious.

"But what if I screw it all up? I've been doing that my entire life," Hunter said.

"Then you screw it up. That doesn't mean you shouldn't take a chance. How do you feel about her?"

Hunter thought about it for a few moments. "I enjoy being with her and I'm in a rush to get back to her. But she's as guarded as me. There's a lot of history between the two of us."

"I never thought I could want anything more than I wanted to make the next big deal," Gabe told him. "Then I met a woman who I thought was completely wrong for me, and I found that I hadn't really known anything at all. She grounds me and makes me free at the same time."

"That makes no sense," Hunter told him.

"Shut up, I'm being serious here," Gabe growled.

"I know. It's just not an easy conversation to have."

"You have to accept what's going on and then let everything else go," Gabe told him.

"I don't think I'm ready to do that," Hunter admitted.

"Then you aren't ready. Maybe you have to accept that too," Gabe said.

"So basically you're telling me to figure it out," Hunter said with a laugh.

"You've never been one to be told what to do, Hunter. That won't change even if you do fall in love. I think you need to finish this mission Dad sent you on, then maybe you'll have the rest of the answers too."

"Maybe. I'm almost afraid for it to end," Hunter said.

"Maybe that's a clue in itself," Gabe told him.

They sat back and Hunter wondered at how much his twin had changed in the past few months. It seemed that he and all his siblings were going through changes. Hunter just couldn't determine if those changes were a good thing or not.

Chapter Eighteen

REBEKAH THREW THE last of her clothes into a bag, and marveled at the pounding of her heart. She didn't understand why she was so anxious about going to another place on the journey for Hunter's treasure. Sure the two of them had been closer in the past week than she'd ever imagined them being, and because of that she'd discovered she had far stronger feelings for Hunter than she cared to admit, but this was just one more step on their journey. It wasn't a big deal.

"Are you ready to go?" Hunter asked as he leaned in the doorjamb.

The man took her breath away. It didn't matter how many times she was around him, it was the same each time. She wished she could be harder, but maybe it was time to give up on that. It just wasn't who she was.

"Yes. I appreciate you bringing me here," she told him. It was strange to have Hunter in the place she'd once thought so safe.

The apartment was tiny, but it had been her home for years. With him there with her, she realized how empty the place actually was.

She didn't have the usual knickknacks lying around that most people accumulated through the years. She had books and more books covering her shelves and that was about all.

"We aren't in a hurry if you want to stay a while," he told her, not moving from his place in her doorway.

The look in his eyes told her exactly what was on his mind. Her body reacted just how she expected it to — instant heat and longing.

"We need to get to the resort, don't we?" she asked.

He chuckled in the doorway. "Don't look so frightened. I'm not going to attack," he said as he licked his lips in a way that sent her need to molten levels. "Unless that's what you want."

Yes! She wanted. She wanted. But the professor part of her brain told her there was more to life than just sex. At the moment she just couldn't seem to figure out exactly what that was.

"I'm ready to go," she told him, her words coming out too breathy, but she stayed focused on her bag instead of him.

"Too bad. But there are more adventures in store," he said as he pushed off the doorjamb and moved over to her bed. He ran his fingers along her comforter, looking directly into her eyes. The heat flaring between them was enough to ignite the apartment, but then he grabbed her bag and left her bedroom.

Rebekah took several moments to compose herself. She looked around at her lifeless apartment before following him to her front door and locking it behind them.

She knew their journey was coming to an end. She wanted so desperately to relish their last bit of time together, but she didn't know how to let her guard all the way down. Maybe it was better that way.

Hunter kept her engaged in small talk on their way to the airport where his private plane awaited them. She knew she was in for a long ride, the two of them being pressed close to each other, but she wasn't afraid of that. She found she would miss it when this was all over. There was such freedom in being in the air with this man as he masterfully controlled a machine most people couldn't even begin to grasp how to run.

There was nothing about Hunter she didn't appreciate or desire. Well, maybe that wasn't true. She didn't appreciate his ability to stick around only long enough for the two of them to see they have something special together. But that was just their fate, she decided.

"Are you ready to see the place my brother Luke inherited?" Hunter asked her after they were up in the sky.

"I have always loved Yosemite Valley," she told him. "I've never been to this resort before."

"My dad bought it a couple years ago. It was where he met my mother for the first time and when it was going under, he wanted to save it," Hunter told her.

"Your father sounds like a sentimental man," she said.

Hunter was quiet for a moment and she wondered if she'd said something wrong. In the small space of the plane, through their headphones, she clearly heard his sigh as a smile appeared on his lips.

"I never would have thought so. He always seemed so hard to me. My mom died when we were all really young. She was the free spirit, the one who held us all together. But then Dad died and he left us all these strange legacies. I guess I've learned more about the man in death than in life. I don't understand it," Hunter told her.

"I think sometimes it's incredibly hard for us to show our true feelings," Rebekah told him. She couldn't help but reach out and touch him in a comforting way.

"I don't understand why," he said. "I thought I wanted nothing to do with my family, that they were nothing more than anchors there to hold me under. But I've talked more to my brothers in the last few months than I have in years. And our dad," he paused as he took in a deep breath. "Our dad might not have been the bastard I thought he was."

"Everyone has layers to them. Sometimes it takes strength to look beneath," she said quietly.

He turned and looked at her, and she felt so exposed in that moment that she wanted to take it back, but she couldn't. The more she was with this man — her first and only love — the more she wanted to thank his father for bringing them together. She didn't know how this journey would end, but she knew she was growing as a person because of it.

"Do you want to see beneath my layers?" he asked her.

"Yes," she said without thinking.

"You might be the only one who can," he told her.

Rebekah didn't know what to say about that. This was the most real conversation the two of them had ever shared and it scared her, but also thrilled her. Could it be that Hunter truly had changed? Maybe they both had.

Before Rebekah was able to respond to his last comment, he pointed out some mountains in the distance. They were getting closer to Luke's resort. Maybe it was better this way. Maybe they didn't need to continue down the road they were on. It didn't feel that way, though. She felt like it was an opportunity missed.

Hunter began to navigate the plane to the runway up ahead and Rebekah's throat hurt from holding back all she wanted to say to him. Time was running out; that she was certain about.

Chapter Nineteen

IFE MOVES FORWARD no matter how hard you try to slow it down. That was a truth Hunter had learned long ago. He'd always appreciated the course of action taken by a person that led someone from one journey to the next. He'd never been happy simply sitting and watching the world go by.

Even knowing this, he wanted to slow time down and take in every moment with Becka. He wanted to show her his world and learn more about hers. He wanted to know if they could merge together — he was afraid he was too hardened to do just that.

It was odd for him to be feeling this way as they drove in silence to the Algoma Resort in Yosemite Valley. He hadn't been there since the last family vacation they'd taken while his mother was still alive. That time had been magical, and there was pain in his gut as he drove beneath the iron archway that led to the place now owned by his brother Luke.

At least he got a little bit more time with Becka as the seemingly endless driveway wound through the area. The resort was set back for maximum privacy and stunning views. He couldn't help but think of the last time he'd been on this very road, in a vehicle with his father who had been such a different man then, one who'd actually smiled and laughed and seemed to enjoy spending time with his wife and sons.

"I love horses," Becka gasped as she gazed out her window, trying to take it all in. "This place is stunning."

Hunter tried to see it through her eyes. He'd grown up in a world of wealth and privilege and somewhere along the line, he had stopped seeing the beauty around him unless he was looking through his pricey camera lenses.

He was envious of what Becka could see — envious of the joy she came by so naturally. He followed her gaze and looked out at the horses running in the meadow.

"This place has it all," he told her.

"Like what?" she asked, her lips turned up as she strained to see everything.

"There's the main lodge, cabins along the river, fishing, rafting, horseback riding. I can't remember it all, it's been so long since I've been here. I don't even know what kind of shape it's in," he said.

They turned a corner and the three-story manor house was front and center ahead of them. The building was huge, and there were a few people wandering about, giving life to the lodge even in the wintertime. It wasn't as busy as it would be during the summer, but with the anticipation of spring in the air, people were beginning to come around for the many adventures the place offered. Luke had filled him in on the changes he and the manger, his fiancée, had been making to the place.

It was so odd how much Luke had changed. Hunter almost felt betrayed by it. After all, he and his brother were the ones who'd set out to seek adventure, to find excitement in all corners of the world. And now Luke was domesticated. It was odd.

This place had once been such an adventure for the whole family to partake in, and now both of his parents were gone. Hunter wondered if being there was going to mess with his head. He decided he wouldn't stick around long enough to allow it. Why had his father put a clue in this particular place? Probably to inspire the emotion Hunter was currently feeling — emotion he wanted nothing to do with.

"This place is truly amazing, Hunter. I think I could stay forever," Becka said as he stopped his car and sat there. He didn't want to get out of the car and leave their cocoon. The reasons why were beyond him.

But Becka pushed open her door, leaving him no choice but to follow her.

"Yeah, we definitely had some adventures here when we were young," he told her. She stopped and looked at him, too much knowledge in her eyes.

Hunter wasn't sure who was more shocked when she stepped up and threw her arms around him. He stood there stiffly for a moment before his arms wrapped around her and he clung on tight. It was odd how comforted he felt by the gesture.

"I'm sorry if this is hard on you," she said, her words muffled against his chest. He let up on some of the pressure. He'd been holding on to her for dear life. Was she his anchor in the storm? That was a humbling thought.

"Looks like we'll be placing you two in Cabin Eleven," Luke said, making Hunter look up to find Luke and Lizzie standing on the huge wraparound porch in front of the lodge's main doors.

"Hello, Brother," Hunter said. He pulled away from Becka, but kept an arm around her, unwilling to let go completely. "Good to see you."

Luke laughed as he looked at both of them. "It seems you only have eyes for one person. I'm surprised you can focus on me," Luke said. He and Lizzie stepped off the porch and moved down to them.

"I'm Lizzie," the woman said as she held out her hand to Becka. "I'm so glad you're here."

"Rebekah," Becka said as she shook Lizzie's hand. "Thanks for having us."

There was a moment of somewhat awkward silence. Luke laughed, leaned in, and gave Hunter a half-hug. Hunter really was changing. It was much easier for him to show affection with his siblings now without the world falling down around him.

"Yep, definitely Cabin Eleven. There's magic in that one," Luke said.

"What in the hell are you talking about?" Hunter asked. Becka was blushing next to him as she scooted a little closer.

"You'll figure it out," Luke told him. "Think you can pry yourself away from your woman long enough for me to show you what we've been doing around here?"

Hunter wanted to tell his brother she wasn't *really* his woman, but he knew that would be a lie. She belonged to him in a way that transcended time and place, and he just as much belonged to her. It was strange to realize that.

"I'm surprised you haven't run the place into the ground yet. You and I aren't exactly known for our business abilities," Hunter said.

"We've managed to run our careers just fine. This was just another step on the journey. Guess Dad knew a little bit about us after all," Luke told him.

"I'm beginning to wonder," Hunter replied before he turned toward Becka. "Do you mind exploring with Lizzie while I go for a walk with Luke?" He realized if she said she was uncomfortable with that, he wouldn't leave her. She really did have power over him.

"Not at all, that sounds great," Becka said. She seemed nervous, but not afraid.

"I'll take her to the cabin and she can get settled," Lizzie offered.

"We're in one cabin?" Becka asked.

"It's the only one available. We're doing a special package this weekend and it's only available because we save that one for family," Lizzie said.

"Oh, uh, okay," Becka stuttered.

Hunter let out a breath of relief. He didn't want them in separate quarters. Hell, he didn't want to be away from her at all.

"They're good. Let's go," Luke told him with a knowing laugh that made Hunter want to clock his brother.

They walked away from the girls as Luke chattered about some of the changes he'd made at the resort. A couple was down at the river fishing with their kids, and another couple was getting a horseback riding lesson, while a bunch of teens were off to the side playing a game of volleyball.

"You've done well here, Luke," Hunter told him. "How can you stand to stay in one place though?" he asked as they made a circle and came around to the back of the lodge, where a huge fire pit sat.

"I didn't think I could," Luke told him. "But the thought of not being with Lizzie is unbearable. And now I'm responsible for her niece, Kaitlyn, as well. I love them both. That's what makes it possible."

"But to sit in one place…" Hunter said again.

"I don't. When Kaitlyn isn't in school we will go on adventures. I just won't do it alone anymore."

"Not ever?" Hunter questioned.

"Sometimes I'll need to take quick trips, but I find that I want them to be with me."

"What in the hell has happened to you?" Hunter asked.

"Are you afraid it's happening to you as well?" Luke asked. The seriousness in his brother's tone scared him more than if he were kidding around.

"Yes," he admitted.

"You can't force it, Hunter. Dad sent us all on these missions, gave us a final legacy in life. What it means is different for all of us, but he knew me better than I realized and I have more respect for the man than I thought would be possible. I miss him — wish I could thank him."

"He didn't even give us a chance to tell him goodbye. We don't owe him anything," Hunter said with anger.

"He gave us everything. We just have to open our eyes to see it," Luke said.

"I don't know if I like this new you," Hunter grumbled.

Luke laughed. "Hell, it took me a while to get used to it too. If I get too annoying, just push me off a cliff."

Hunter finally laughed. "You'd just open a magical parachute, film the entire thing and make a million bucks," Hunter told him. "Don't think I'm helping to boost your fame."

"Looks who's talking. You've taken pictures all over the world. Didn't I read an article in a magazine about one of your signed prints hanging in the president's private living room?"

Hunter shrugged, feeling slightly uncomfortable. It wasn't that he was humble or anything like that, it was just that he tended to take the pictures, send them where they needed to go, and move on to the next adventure. When a staff member had come to him on request from the president and asked him to sign a copy for the big man himself, Hunter had been too shocked to consider refusing. He hadn't told his siblings. They'd found out anyway.

"It could have been taken down by now," Hunter said with a shrug.

"Come on, Brother, don't be getting all modest on me now. It's going to ruin your rugged reputation," Luke said with another laugh. Hunter couldn't remember the last time he'd had such a conversation with any of his brothers, let alone the one he'd competed with most.

"Don't worry. That will never happen," Hunter said as he sat down. "When are you going to get me a beer and light this fire?"

Luke rolled his eyes. "Yes, sir. My aim is to please," Luke told him before he disappeared.

It was odd that his adventurous brother was so settled down that he was actually worried about his guests having a good time. Maybe the world had turned inside out. Hunter knew he certainly had.

Luke returned with the beer and actually did start the fire. As they continued to talk, Hunter relaxed. He stopped trying to analyze everything that was being said, and instead let go and allowed himself to enjoy spending time with his brother. In Hunter's line of work, he didn't allow himself friendships, but the more they talked, the clearer it became to him what a fool he was.

Luke wasn't only his brother, they also had a lot in common and the two of them — hell, his entire family — had wasted a lot of years trying to forge their own paths. Maybe they should have done more together.

"I hope we aren't interrupting, but we brought food," Lizzie said as she stepped out to them and set something delicious-smelling on a nearby table, Becka at her side.

"You could never interrupt," Luke said, grabbing her around the waist and pulling her down into his lap, kissing her with open abandon.

Hunter's gaze met Becka's with so much heat, the fire seemed cold in comparison. Her eyes dilated as she took a step toward him. He was more than ready to find that cabin.

"Eat first. You'll need it," Luke said with another laugh. Hunter broke his gaze with Becka and took his first breath in several moments. Then he laughed with Luke.

"Are you a mind reader now?" Hunter asked.

"Hard not to read your mind when the sparks are flying so high you're about to start a forest fire."

"Let's eat then. It's been a long day and I'm ready for bed," Hunter said.

Luke laughed. "That sounds like an excellent idea."

It was a quick meal. Hunter was ready to get Becka to this magical cabin he'd been told about. It had already been too long since he'd had her in his arms.

Chapter Twenty

REBEKAH FELT AS if she were floating on clouds as she and Hunter made their way to the cabin. She knew beyond a doubt she didn't want to stop what was about to happen. Maybe it was more than a magical cabin, maybe the entire place was enchanted. She'd been feeling such strong emotion from the moment this trip had begun and she didn't want to fight it anymore.

Not a word was spoken as they walked inside the small cabin, the bed taking up a lot of the space. They didn't need anything more. Hunter looked into her eyes and she was lost to anything but him as he pulled her close and touched her lips with so much compassion it felt almost like love.

Their clothes melted away as he lay her down on the bed, then stood there for several moments gazing at her. Rebekah felt a tinge of embarrassment, a need to cover herself, but as she looked at his naked body, it was more than obvious how much he desired her. There was no reason for her to hide.

He joined her on the bed and a moan escaped her lips as he skimmed his fingers across her stomach, slowly moving higher to brush her breasts. He barely touched her and her heart thundered, her breath halted and her core heated.

Letting go of her worries and focusing only on Hunter and the pleasure he brought to her was all she could do. She needed him — wanted him — lusted for only his touch. It was just the two of them and nothing else mattered.

He leaned into her and ran his lips across hers — not long enough to satisfy the need within her, but long enough to stoke the flames ever higher. He kissed her cheeks, her neck, her jaw, then moved back to her lips, not connecting them in the way she needed them to connect.

He took his time, his lips and tongue whispering along her skin. She reached for him, tried to hold him in place, but he grabbed her hands and held them above her head as he looked down into her eyes.

"I have all night," he promised, making her squirm beneath him.

"I want you now," she told him.

"I want you always," he replied before lazily running his lips across hers.

He moved his hands and she tried to reach for him, but couldn't. Her eyes snapped open as she realized he'd tied them to the headboard.

"What are you doing?" she asked with a mixture of excitement and wonder.

"Anything I want," he replied as he kissed her again.

"What if I want to do things?" she asked as she struggled against her binds. She wasn't in too big of a hurry to escape though, not with him touching her like this.

"I'll give you plenty of opportunities," he told her.

Rebekah couldn't remember ever being this excited. She fully trusted Hunter. There was nothing he would do to her that she didn't love, didn't crave. She wiggled beneath him, aching even more.

He scooted to the side of her and ran his palms from her breasts to the top of her core and back again. She arched against his touch, needing him to give her more. His hands made several more passes on her body before he leaned down and ran his tongue over her peaked nipple.

She cried out at the beautiful ache he was building within her. His lips circled her nipple and he sucked, making her core pulse as she sought sweet relief. He licked the nipple again before moving back to her neck and sucking.

"Are you pleased, Becka?" he whispered, his hot breath washing over her ear.

"Yes, but I want more," she whimpered.

"What do you want?" he asked as he moved back down and sucked her other nipple, making her back arch off the bed.

"That," she told him before another moan escaped.

"Only this?" he asked, sucking harder.

"No. I want it all," she said.

His fingers moved down her stomach and brushed between her spread thighs. She jumped as heat flooded her and she felt herself grow even wetter.

He kissed his way down her stomach and she felt his hot breath on her core, felt his light kisses. It still wasn't enough. She arched toward his mouth but he just skimmed his lips where she wanted them pressed.

"Please, Hunter, please," she begged.

He ran his tongue on the outside of her folds, and she panted as he played her body like a musician would an instrument. Then he moved and kissed her thighs, making her groan in disapproval. She wanted him touching her in one place only and she was ready to beg if that's what he demanded.

"Please, Hunter, you know what I need," she told him, struggling against the binds at her wrists.

Her body pulsed with every touch of his tongue and fingers. Then he was finally where she needed him the most. A cry escaped as his lips clamped down on the swollen flesh of her core. He sucked as his tongue circled her pulsing skin.

"Yes ... yes ... yes," she called out over and over again. He sucked harder as he dipped a finger inside her wet flesh.

It took only seconds before she went up in flames, her body clenching as a beautiful orgasm ripped through her. He continued sucking her sensitive flesh, making her scream in pleasure and pain. He didn't stop until the last of her quivers stopped. Then he ran his tongue along her folds, making her shake beneath him.

Hunter kissed his way back up her body, his tongue circling her breasts before he kissed her arms then undid the ties holding her. She immediately reached for him, her fingers clenching in his hair as she felt the weight of him on top of her.

She was exhausted but as he pressed against her, she felt desire stirring again, building, heating, readying her for him.

"Take me, Hunter," she said on a sigh as he leaned down and kissed her, his tongue sinking into her mouth as he slowly began pressing inside her body with his thick, hot steel.

"Oh, that's so good," she said as she threw her head back, enjoying every delectable inch of him pushing inside her. "So hard ..."

She could barely utter words, but she had to tell him how she was feeling. She was so full, so happy. She could lie this way with him forever and be in perfect bliss.

He rested when he was fully sheathed inside her. She enjoyed the moment for a few seconds longer and then she wanted movement.

"Take me, Hunter. I want you to take me hard," she demanded. Her body was hot and ready and she wanted another release. She wanted it with him. She wrapped her legs around his back, digging into him with her heels as she pushed against him.

"Yes, baby, I want you," he said on a growl.

He grabbed her butt and pulled out, then slammed hard against her, shaking the bed in his force.

"Yes, more," she demanded.

Their cries were mingled in the air with the sound of their bodies slapping together. He groaned as he picked up speed, taking her faster and harder as she cried out, her stomach tight, her core clenching around him.

And then she let go, shaking as her orgasm exploded through her. He made a guttural sound as she tightened around him and he slammed deep within her, his body pulsing and tense. They basked in the pleasure as both of them shook for endless moments in time.

Rebekah was exhausted, but she still didn't want to let Hunter go — she never wanted to let him go. She was only truly home when he was buried deep inside her. It's where they should always be.

"You're mine, Becka," he said as he pulled from her. Emptiness filled her at the disconnect and she reached for him.

"Always," she whispered and he pulled her to his side — right where she belonged.

Chapter Twenty-One

REBEKAH WOKE UP to the smell of coffee, and the first thing she saw was Hunter sitting at the small table in the corner of the cabin. He was concentrating on the paper in front of him and she took a moment to study him, to appreciate the beauty of the man. Not making a sound, she watched him as he picked up his coffee cup and took a sip.

She was tired, as the two of them had spent half the night making love, but it had been well worth it. She couldn't seem to turn him down when she woke up with his hands and lips roaming across her body. She would take what she could get during the limited time they had left together.

She didn't make a sound, but still he turned, his eyes connecting with hers. For a moment there was such softness there that she melted back against the bed, wanting to open her arms for him to come to her. How she could possibly even think about making love again, she wasn't sure, but it wasn't an unpleasant thought.

"Good morning," he said in a voice that had her all tingly and warm.

"Morning," she replied.

"I have your coffee," he said as he rose and poured her a cup, adding just the right amount of sugar and cream.

She sat up in bed, the blankets held in place by her arms as she accepted the cup. Her first sip was heaven. He leaned down and brushed her lips before sitting on the edge of the bed.

"Hope you slept well."

"Mmm, I seem to recall being woken up several times," she told him.

He brushed her hair from her face as he smiled at her. Hunter was an intense man in every aspect of his life, but for this frozen moment in time, he looked utterly relaxed, and she felt peace at how perfect they were together.

That made Becka wonder how one day, or to be even more specific, one moment could be so right, and then how it could all go so very wrong in the next. Why didn't people hold onto these moments, cherish them and never let them go? Was it pride that stood in their way? Maybe. Humans were foolish. An animal would never let something insignificant grow to the point that the situation was irreversible.

Sometimes things were truly out of a person's hands, and other times it would only take a kind word, a gesture of love or loyalty to make everything alright. Was Rebekah strong enough to be that person, willing to risk it all? She didn't know.

"I can't seem to get enough of you. I hope you feel the same way," he told her.

"Oh, I definitely feel the same," she said. "But we do have a busy day so I should finish this coffee, shower, and put some clothes on."

"I don't think you ever need to wear clothes," he said.

She chuckled. "It might be awkward visiting with your brother stark naked. His fiancée might have a problem with it."

Hunter's eyes dilated at just the thought of that and she relished in his jealousy.

"You're absolutely right. You're only allowed to be naked when we're alone," he said. He pulled the blanket away from her chest and her nipples instantly peaked from his hungry look.

He bent down and ran his tongue over one and then the other. Rebekah forgot all about what they had to do for the day. He could have her anytime he wanted and she was perfectly okay with that. When he leaned back and looked at her wet chest and her hungry eyes, his own were dilated, dark and sexy.

"I don't understand this pull you have over me," he said as he reached for her, his fingers dancing on her skin.

"It goes both ways," she assured him.

He leaned in again as she set her coffee cup aside, better desires awakened than the need for coffee, food, or a shower. But then there was a knock on the door.

"They'll go away," he told her, his mouth latching onto her breast again. She hoped he was right.

"It's ten, Hunter. Let go of the girl and get your ass out here."

"Luke," Hunter growled as he let her go. She whimpered before she was able to stop it and he smiled at her. "At least I'll know how hungry you're going to be for me all day," he whispered before he covered her back up and stood.

Hunter moved to the door and cracked it open to peer at his brother, who Rebekah couldn't see.

"I'm coming out. Move away from the door," Hunter told him.

Rebekah heard Luke laugh, then heard his steps retreating from the doorway. Hunter turned back to look at her.

"Don't take too long or I'll have to come back in and finish what we started. To hell with Luke," he said.

She wasn't sure if he was kidding or not, but as soon as the door to the cabin was safely shut, she jumped up and turned the lock. As much as she would love to make love with Hunter again, she didn't relish the thought of doing so with an audience on the other side of the walls.

Her body ached as she turned the water on high in the shower. She might have bended in ways she'd never tried before during the night. Lovemaking with Hunter was new and exciting each time. It had been the same for them ten years ago. He knew how to please a woman — that much hadn't changed.

She dressed for adventure since they'd be searching for the next clue in Hunter's legacy. Though she was feeling much better after her snakebite, she still didn't want to push herself too hard. Hunter had promised this wouldn't be a hike through the mountains or anything. At least she had that to be grateful for.

Stepping outside, Rebekah didn't find Hunter or his brother, so she made her way up the trails to the main lodge and stepped inside. Lizzie had already given her the full tour, but it was still fascinating to see all the people milling about. And Lizzie had told her this wasn't even their busy season.

She made her way to the dining hall and found Lizzie sitting at a table with another woman and an adorable baby. She walked over to the group.

"You're just in time for breakfast," Lizzie told her as she pushed out a chair. "Join us. This is my head cook and very good friend, Shari Jordan and her baby girl, Julia."

"It's a pleasure to meet you," Rebekah said, but her eyes were for the child only. Her womb seemed to twitch as she gazed down at the smiling face.

"Do you want to hold her?" Shari asked.

"Yes," Rebekah said.

Lizzie and Shari chuckled. "She has that effect on people. The guests adore her," Shari assured Rebekah as she handed over the sweet baby girl.

"Are you getting any ideas?" she heard Luke ask with a laugh.

Rebekah looked up to see Hunter and Luke walking up to the table. Hunter's eyes were on her and she could swear she saw a bit of panic there. She realized seeing her with the baby was a huge red flag for him. It broke her heart in ways she hadn't even realized she'd opened it up for breaking.

"No, no ideas here," Hunter said, a forced laugh escaping him.

"Yeah, okay," Luke said as he pulled another chair over and sat down next to his fiancee. "Better get some food so you can get to work for Daddy," he teased.

"Yeah, you jumped through the old man's hoops first," Hunter pointed out.

The baby began to fuss, and Rebekah was glad to give her back. With Hunter there seeming so uncomfortable, she was nervous holding the child, which is probably why she had gone from smiley to fussy in an instant.

Their breakfast was quiet and the more time that passed, the more uncomfortable Rebekah began to feel. Their night and morning had been so ideal, and now there was this weird awkwardness between them. She didn't like it — not one little bit. Maybe the two of them should have just stayed in bed all day like she'd originally thought.

"Time to go," Hunter said, and Rebekah gave up on eating. Her stomach was too tied up in knots.

"Okay." She stood up and thanked Luke and Lizzie for a wonderful meal before she followed Hunter from the lodge. "Where are we going?"

"Luke told me the way. I couldn't figure out the map but when I showed him, he just laughed and said he knew exactly where the next clue would be located."

"Is it far?" she asked as he took her around a corner where a golf cart was waiting. She eyed it skeptically.

"No, not too far," he told her.

He was so cold all of a sudden, she didn't know what to think about it. Maybe all good things really did come to an end, or maybe he was just having an off moment and she was reading too much into it.

Still, it was odd that they were so silent as he steered the golf cart around the property. They went up into the trees and after about ten minutes he stopped and got out.

"We're here," he said. There was a tightness in his voice she didn't understand.

"Are you okay?" she asked.

He quietly walked up to a tree and ran his fingers over the bark. That's when she saw what he was looking at. She felt tears spring to her eyes. "Colin loves Kathleen" was carved inside of a heart.

"That's your mother and father, isn't it?" she asked, remembering his father's name was Colin.

"Yeah. I didn't even know this was here. When Luke and I looked at the map together he told me Lizzie had shown him the tree, that it would be the most fitting place for our father to have left the next clue."

The two of them glanced down at a small marker in the ground. Most people wouldn't have noticed it, but since they'd been treasure hunting for a while now, they knew what to look for.

"He must have really loved your mother," Rebekah said.

"Yeah, more than I ever realized," Hunter told her. "Lizzie told my brother the story of how they came to be, how they'd met right here at the lodge and then parted ways, but my father apparently said that fate brought them back together again when they met back up in Kentucky ten years later."

"That's pretty romantic," Rebekah told him. She couldn't help but see the parallel to her own story with Hunter.

"I can't imagine it. I can't see that side of my father, but the proof seems to be everywhere we look," he told her with a sigh.

"I'm sorry this is so hard on you, Hunter," she told him. She finally found the courage to move up beside him and place her hand on his arm.

"It's not hard," he said, but his voice contradicted his words.

"Okay," she said, humoring him.

"I'll get the shovel."

Hunter pulled from her touch, and she felt the chill in the air all the way through her bones as he moved back to the golf cart and pulled out the shovel. He came back and immediately began digging where the marker was.

It didn't take him long to hit a plastic box. He dug it out and brushed off the dirt then walked back over to the golf cart, Rebekah at his side. Was this the final clue? Was their journey over? She felt on the verge of tears as she waited to see what it was.

Hunter finally opened the box. Inside was a single piece of paper, bearing a final map and a poem:

I've brought you to a place of love
To show you the magic of it all.
Where once there was dark
Light was found.
But most don't have the courage
To hold on like they should.
You've come near and far while seeking treasure.
The only hope is that it has brought you truth.
Go back home and you will find
The end of the way is on the hills where it all began.
This journey must come to a close
With your guide by your side.

Chapter Twenty-Two

S AYING GOODBYE TO Luke and Lizzie, Hunter and Rebekah left the lodge with barely a look behind them. She could have easily stayed for days longer, at least one more night in the cabin that had turned out to be magical after all. But once Hunter had his clue in hand, he'd been ready to go — ready to finish his treasure hunt.

Now Rebekah didn't have to wonder when it would all be finished. She knew. There was one more location for them to go, then it was over. She wanted to know where they would be, but wasn't sure how to broach the subject.

They arrived back at the plane, and it didn't take long to load up their bags and complete Hunter's pre-flight checklist. The anticipation Rebekah usually felt when she got to fly with Hunter wasn't there. She was too uncertain to feel anything other than dread at the moment. Still, she couldn't take the silence for very long.

"We only have one more clue left. I bet you're excited," she said about fifteen minutes into the flight.

"It will be nice to quit chasing after whatever it is my father needs me to find," Hunter told her.

"All the same, I've had fun doing it with you, though I'm sure you would have been fine on your own," she told him. She forced a laugh, and it sounded awkward through the headphones they were wearing.

"I've enjoyed you being here with me," he told her. Then he sighed.

"Whatever it is you need to say to me, I would rather you spit it out instead of sitting there all broody like you've been all day," Rebekah said. They weren't looking at each other, but their bodies were pressed close in the small plane and there was nowhere for either of them to escape to unless one of them planned on jumping for it. It was actually something Hunter might be willing to do.

"I'm sorry," Hunter told her as he reached out and put his hand on her leg. She hadn't realized how much she'd needed his touch until she had it again. She let out a bit of a relieved sigh. She began to feel a stirring of hope.

"It's okay. But I would rather you tell me when something is wrong," she said.

He sighed again and she knew he hadn't been apologizing about his mood. Something else was going on and she was sure she wouldn't like whatever it was.

"I got a call after I left the cabin this morning," he began. Her stomach tightened. This wasn't going to be a phone call she was going to like.

"Phone calls don't normally put someone in such a brooding mood," she said, trying desperately to inject a sense of humor into her voice.

"It's about a job," he said quietly.

Rebekah's heart stalled as she took in what he was saying. If it was one of his jobs, that meant he'd be leaving — probably the country — and it also meant the end of the two of them.

"That's great," she said, refusing to allow tears into her voice. "What sort of job is it?"

"Taking photos," he said, his voice devoid of emotion.

"I figured that," she told him. "Of what?"

Silence stretched between them and she waited for the bomb to drop. This was the slowest a Band-Aid had ever been ripped off, and she wanted that final piece torn away.

"It's a place in Korea," he finally said.

"Wow, that must be exciting," she pushed out. It wasn't how she felt at all, but what else could she say? Yes, they'd been intimate with each other, but they had no level of commitment. She'd always known at the end of the treasure hunt he would leave. It was just that for a short time she'd allowed herself to forget.

"I don't know if I'm taking the job," he said, another sound escaping him.

"Why wouldn't you?" she asked.

"Because of you," he admitted. That hope Rebekah had been trying to keep tampered down was blooming in her chest. She didn't want to lose control of her emotions, but with those three little words, he'd cracked open her heart.

"I don't want to hold you back, Hunter. I don't want you to resent me," she said. It would be worse for her to keep him, knowing he resented her for it, than to let him go and deal with the loss.

"I would never think of you that way. My life has never been planned out. I've always taken each new day as it comes. But being with you again has changed how I feel. I don't know if I'm ready to let that go," he told her.

She desperately wanted to look in his eyes, but she was afraid to do it. What did all of this mean? He wasn't exactly telling her he wanted forever, but he was saying he didn't want to leave. But was that for now? Or was it for a few more days, weeks, possibly even months? This uncertainty wasn't something she would wish on anyone.

"I'm here. There's nowhere I need to go," she finally said. She was letting him know she was here if he wanted her. She felt too vulnerable, but she would hate herself if she didn't say it, didn't tell him.

He squeezed her thigh as they drew closer to the airport and he began their approach.

"I know you are," he finally said, his voice just above a whisper.

They touched down and taxied in. No more was said as the two of them exited the plane, put it away, and then placed their things in his car. He opened her door and finally, she took a deep breath. It was now or never.

"Can we not think about any of this for now?" she said. He looked at her with a bit of shock. "I just want to spend the night together. We'll complete the treasure hunt tomorrow."

Hunter's eyes glazed over and he pulled her against him, his hands wrapping behind her back.

"Yes." It was one simple word, but it was everything for her. For tonight they had no problems. For tonight he was hers, and she was his. Tomorrow they might take a new path, but tonight was all theirs.

Chapter Twenty-Three

REBEKAH WASN'T SURE if the night before had been her last with Hunter, but as they followed the dirt road up into the hills of Hunter's brother's property on dirt bikes, she knew something was about to happen.

They were reaching the final clue in their short journey together. He hadn't told her if he was taking the job that would pull him out of her life again, and she hadn't wanted to talk about it. All she'd wanted the night before was to be lost in his arms. They'd made such sweet love she'd ached after as she'd laid in his arms.

When she'd been sure he was asleep, she'd finally snuck off into the bathroom and let the tears she'd been fighting all day slip freely down her face. Once that had been done, she'd cleaned herself up, then crawled back into his arms and fallen asleep.

They'd had normal chitchat all morning, then it had been time to go. She hadn't rode a dirt bike in a long time, but quickly got the hang of it again and felt free as they climbed the mountain in search of the final place on their treasure hunt.

When Hunter stopped his bike, she pulled up beside him and turned off the engine. The quiet was almost eerie as the two of them dismounted and moved into the trees. Several paces in, Hunter stopped.

Rebekah felt a sense of restlessness as they gazed at the large tree in front of them, a marker at its base. Carved into the bark was a heart with nothing in it. She wasn't sure what that meant. Had someone just grown tired of carving?

"Looks like we found the place," Hunter said with a sardonic smile.

"Seems so," she told him.

He pulled the small shovel from his backpack and stood there, looking like he was in no hurry to end their journey. She wasn't either, but she knew they had to finish, so she took the shovel from him and dug until they found the same type of plastic box they'd seen at the resort.

Hunter finally moved into action and dug it the rest of the way out. He carried it over to a sun-soaked patch of grass where wildflowers, urged on by the light filtering through the trees, had begun to sprout up.

He ran his hands over the top of the small box, and her heart pounded as she waited for him to open it. He didn't say anything; he just sat there gazing at the box.

"The anticipation is killing me," she finally told him.

He let out a sound that resembled a laugh. But her words spurred him into motion. He moved his fingers to the latch and opened the box. Rebekah peered inside, where what appeared to be a jewelry box and an envelope rested.

He took out the jewelry case and set it aside without opening it, then picked up the envelope. He looked at her and there was such an innocent look in his eyes, it broke her heart. He seemed so lost.

"This is it," he said. "This is the final clue from my dad."

His voice cracked on the last word and she felt so much compassion for him that she couldn't help but move over and climb into his lap, throwing her arms around him.

"I'm here with you," she assured him.

"I'm glad you are," he told her. His hand rubbed her back. They sat that way for several minutes before she moved off him so he could take the final step in this journey.

"Would you rather I leave you to do this alone?" she asked.

"No. I want you here," he said.

Finally, he cracked the envelope and Rebekah found herself trembling as she waited to see what the letter said. She'd always wanted to go on a treasure hunt, and now she didn't think she would be able to suffer through one again. She was far too emotional to deal with the anticipation of it all.

Finally he read the letter, leaving it open for her to see as well.

You have been put through a lot to come to the end of this hunt to receive your legacy, but it has happened because you are the wanderer of the family. The hope of this task is for you to realize you don't have to be far from home to have adventures. You can have it all, an exciting life that also includes a great love and the support of your brothers.

No one has to be alone, and they shouldn't be. Too many become broken and bitter by choosing that lonely path. Hopefully, you will make changes in your life to set your path straight before that happens to you. May your brothers and you find peace and happiness.

The family attorney has permission to give you the deed to your new home when you present this letter. It's only five miles down the road from your beloved twin brother. You boys need each other and putting down roots doesn't make you less of a man, it gives you a foundation that will give you strength the rest of your life. The second part of your legacy is within the black jewelry box. May you have the strength to know what to do with it. You are wise and you have been lost. Know that home is always where you can be found again.

"Is it from your father?" Rebekah asked, tears streaming down her cheeks.

Hunter looked at the letter, front and back, a frown on his face. Rebekah was afraid to know what was in the jewelry case, but she was also hopeful. This was the end of the treasure hunt, but Hunter's father had obviously meant it to be the beginning of his son's journey in life.

"I don't know," he said with a sigh. "It's not signed, just like everything else."

"You can choose to believe it's from him," she told him.

He gave her the semblance of a smile. "It doesn't sound like something he would write," he told her.

"I don't believe that. It sounds like there were many layers to your dad that you weren't able to see when he was still alive. It seems he loved your mother very much and he only wants you and your brothers to have the same thing," she said.

"I don't know," he repeated. She desperately wanted to hold him.

Hunter set down the letter and picked up the jewelry box. He opened the lid and found an antique wedding ring inside, the diamonds glittering in the sun, taking Rebekah's breath away. Their gazes met and she didn't know how to read the look in his eyes.

"This was my grandmother's," Hunter said. He ran his finger over the center diamond. Rebekah held her breath. She knew in that moment if he wanted her forever, she was his.

But she saw the shutters close over his eyes and she knew this wasn't where his journey was going to take him. He wasn't ready for it. She'd learned more from this treasure hunt than he had. For him, it really had been about getting to the end. For her, it had made her realize she'd never fallen out of love with him, that she wanted a future with this man that included roots and babies.

But she could wait forever and still never have it.

"It's okay, Hunter," she told him. A few more tears slipped.

"Becka," he said. Her name came out as an apology. She hurt so much right now, but what she hated even more was that *he* was hurting too. He'd never meant for things to go this far. He loved her as much as he was capable of loving. At least *that* she would be able to carry with her during all the lonely nights sure to come.

"It's okay," she repeated. She leaned against him and kissed him for a final time. "You found what you needed to find. I'm glad I was here for you. I'm going to let you absorb it all."

He grabbed her and kissed her hard before letting her go. Rebekah was barely holding it together. She stood and walked back to her bike. She had to see him one final time though. She turned and he was gazing at the ground, looking lost.

"Goodbye, Hunter."

He looked up and their eyes met. She saw the finality of his decision in his eyes. She couldn't look anymore. She put on her helmet, got on her bike, and she rode away from him. It was over. The journey was over.

Chapter Twenty-Four

HUNTER WAS BACK in town after only a month. And it had still been too long for him to be gone. His heart hadn't been in the project he'd been working on and there hadn't been a single image captured that he'd found good enough to publish. He'd felt lost and out of sorts. Only when he'd landed in California, jumped in his vehicle, and began the familiar drive to the bar his brother Knox worked at in Santa Monica, did he begin to feel normal once more.

He'd told all his brothers he would be there. He guessed it would be a surprise to find out who showed up. When they had all learned of their father's death, they had met up at The Wake for their aunt to pass out their legacies. Hunter hadn't been able to make it that time. He decided from here on out that his family would be a priority for him and not much was going to stop him from seeing his siblings anymore.

The Wake was crowded for a Friday afternoon. Maybe the bar was serving a good lunch special. It had been a while since he'd been in there, but some greasy fries didn't sound too bad. He made his way through the crowd and found three out of six of his siblings sitting at what had become the family table.

Gabe was there with a burger and fries in front of him and Hunter sat next to him, reaching over and scooping up a handful of the fries.

"I guess what's mine is yours," Gabe said as he looked at Knox with a brow raised.

Knox understood what Gabe wanted. "Yes, I'll have more brought out," Knox told him with a laugh before getting up and placing the order.

"I love it when he obeys," Gabe said with a laugh.

"Don't get used to it. He's been in a mood the past couple weeks," Luke told them.

"What's new about that?" Hunter asked. His handful of fries was empty and he hoped like hell it didn't take long for more. He hadn't felt much like eating during the past month, but being back home had wetted his appetite.

"You can all shut up or get out," Knox said when he returned with a round of beers.

"What happened to the Bushmills 21 single malt?" Gabe grumbled as he accepted a beer.

"It's a working day, isn't it?" Knox pointed out as he looked at Gabe's immaculate suit.

"One whiskey doesn't hurt anything," Gabe said.

"Yeah, but we never stop at one," Luke said with a laugh.

"True," Hunter and Gabe chorused.

"Damn, it's nice to be in the same room with you two. I forgot how much you used to do that," Knox said.

"Do what?" both Gabe and Hunter said before they realized exactly what they'd been doing. Knox and Luke laughed while Hunter shrugged.

"I can't help it if my twin admires me so much he wants to be just like me," Hunter said as he stole more of Gabe's fries.

"I'm the older brother. I think it's the other way around," Gabe pointed out.

Hunter's food arrived and Gabe stole some fries back while Hunter picked up the burger and took a bite before replying.

"It's three freaking minutes and you never let it go," Hunter said.

"I think this is an argument we're going to be hearing until the day you die," Luke said with an eye roll.

"Don't worry. I'll make sure to last at least three minutes longer than Gabe," Hunter assured them all.

"So what did you want us here for?" Knox asked. The bar began clearing out, which must mean lunch was over. Hunter was grateful for the dimming of the chatter.

"Can't I just want to see my brothers?" Hunter asked.

They all looked at him as if he had a screw loose.

"It's not something that's occurred … ever," Knox pointed out.

"Maybe things have changed," Hunter told them. "I just wish the rest could have made it."

"They come more often now," Luke pointed out. "It's just that we're all close by."

"Or that you don't have lives," Hunter said.

"I just closed on a multimillion-dollar deal," Gabe pointed out.

"And I just finished filming in a place you wouldn't even know how to find," Luke told him.

"I'm pretty much here," Knox said with a grin. "And I like it. The ladies are always around."

"I never shared with you what Dad left me," Hunter finally said, putting all kidding aside. The smiles dropped off his brothers' faces as they looked at the letter he placed on the table.

"That's yours, Hunter. You don't have to share," Luke said, though it was more than obvious he wanted to know what it was.

"I think part of our problem has been in not sharing," Hunter admitted. "I allowed Becka to walk away from me after receiving this," he said before pulling out the ring. "And this." He opened the box and set it on top of the letter.

"Is that Grandma's ring?" Knox asked.

"Yeah. Think the old man was trying to tell me something?" Hunter questioned.

"Yeah, maybe a little," Luke said in a quiet voice.

"Why did you let her go?" Gabe asked. Now that Gabe was all whole and in love, he obviously couldn't imagine doing something so foolish.

"Because I'm an idiot," Hunter admitted.

"Are you going to do something about it?" Luke asked. Knox was unusually quiet during the exchange.

"I don't know if it's too late," Hunter said.

Knox grabbed the letter and was the first to read it. Once he did, his other brothers pounced and read it as well. Hunter waited for them to finish, then they all looked at him. He could swear they were as emotional as he was about it, though none of them would dare to admit to that.

"Is it from Dad?" Knox asked quietly.

"I don't think we'll ever know," Hunter told him.

"We can choose to believe it is," Luke said with a sigh.

"I will," Hunter admitted.

"Now what?" Knox asked. It was silent for several moments after those words were spoken. Then Gabe smiled.

"I think you need to go and get the girl," Gabe told him.

"She loves you, Hunter. I saw it when you came to the resort," Luke said.

"What if she says no?" Hunter asked, hating that he sounded so weak.

"Then you change her mind," Knox said with a smile.

Hunter sat back for a moment and then he laughed. Leave it to his brothers to make such a complicated situation so simple. He leaned back and grinned as he finished his beer.

"I think it's time to get the girl."

He stood up and walked from the bar, his brothers catcalling behind him. He had a new mission — and this one ended with the treasure in his arms *and* in his bed for the rest of his life.

Chapter Twenty-Five

REBEKAH HADN'T KNOWN it was possible to feel any more miserable than she had ten years before, when Hunter had walked away from her. Yes, this time she'd been the one to leave, but it was because she'd known he wanted her to. And he hadn't tried to stop her.

It had been a month since she'd last seen him and the pain of loss still sat with her night and day. It was difficult for her to come to school, to teach classes, to see young students so in love and so naïve about the real world. She wanted to tell them pain was coming, but just barely managed to keep herself from shouting it out.

On this particular day her classroom seemed much more restless than normal, with students whispering to each other and sneaking glances at their phones. It was on days like this that she wondered what the point was of trying to teach a bunch of kids who had no desire to learn.

She tried telling herself she loved her job. Normally she did love it — very much —but after her adventures with Hunter, it had been difficult to resume her day-to-day life. At least she'd lost the glasses that annoyed her so much. If her students didn't take her seriously, that was their problem.

She didn't seem to be having issues with that anymore. Maybe it was because in the last few months she'd grown up more than she had in years. Heartbreak had a tendency to do that to a person.

"We have a test coming up next Monday so you might want to start paying attention," Rebekah told her classroom.

The murmurs quieted as she focused on the projector in front of her. She needed to jot a note down for the class she'd just scolded for not listening, but she had no idea what to write. Maybe a lack of sleep and surviving on caffeine alone had finally fried her brain. It was a real possibility.

She heard the beat of quiet music playing over the speaker system, and she looked up in irritation. Had one of the tech students decided to play a prank again? The volume rose, and the class began to giggle.

When Rebekah recognized the song, she looked around, wondering if this was someone's sick idea of a joke. Tears popped into her eyes and then the doors at the top of the classroom opened and Hunter was standing there, a rose in his hand as the music from "Down on Bended Knee" played.

She couldn't hold back her tears as he sang along with the music, walking down the stairs, her classroom chattering as all the kids watched this beautiful man moving toward her, his own eyes glistening.

Can somebody tell me how to get things back to the way it used to be …

He moved closer. She wasn't sure her own legs were going to hold her up. What was he doing? What was he saying? This was just a song, but it was all about asking for forgiveness, asking her to come back to him. Was that what he wanted?

As the song came to its final verse, he reached Rebekah and dropped to his knee before her while the class looked on. There was a hush as the students took in the show. Then Hunter opened his mouth and sang the final verse.

… I'll never walk again until you come back to me, I'm down on bended knees …

The music faded away and Rebekah didn't see the students staring at them, didn't hear their whispers, didn't see the harsh light of the university classroom. All she saw was Hunter in front of her, a rose in one hand, his grandmother's ring in the other, a plea in his eyes.

"I've messed up so many times in my life, but the worst mistake I've ever made was letting you go — and I did it not once, but twice," he told her. He cleared his throat and continued. "I have nothing without you, nothing at all. I should have never let you walk away, but I promise if you take me back, I'll never break your heart again. I'll cherish you, take you on adventures, and be there for you every moment of every day."

He laid the rose at her feet and reached into his jacket, pulling out what looked to be a hastily drawn treasure map. There were trees and buildings and a very poorly drawn chapel in the corner with a big X on it.

"Take this final treasure hunt with me. Be my wife," he said.

"Hunter …" She had to stop and take several breaths through her tears. "I don't know if this is what you really want," she said. She couldn't go through another heartbreak with this man. It would kill her.

"I promise you it's all I want — all I need," he told her. "We've both suffered enough. Let's just love each other."

Rebekah could try to fight this, could list a hundred reasons why it wouldn't work. But the reality was, she loved him, needed him, and didn't want to live her life without him.

"I love you," she told him.

There was a sigh in the classroom that barely registered in Rebekah's love-riddled brain.

"I love you, Becka, more than anything else in this world," he told her.

"Yes … yes," she said, dropping to the ground with him.

Hunter pulled her into his arms and kissed her, taking the last of her pain away. They didn't stop until an eruption of happy applause broke out from her students. She looked up, her cheeks red as she realized what a public display they'd just made. She smiled at Hunter as they both stood. He slipped the ring on her finger, and she was glowing as she turned to face her classroom.

"Well, I guess class is dismissed early and everyone just earned an automatic A on the test on Monday because I won't feel like grading," she said.

Another cheer arose in the classroom and Hunter laughed as he looked down at her. She was so overjoyed she could barely contain it.

"How about we go to your office and make this deal official?" he said with a wicked look in his eyes.

"I thought you'd never ask," she said, her heart filled with joy.

He picked her up caveman-style, much to the joy of the class, and Rebekah's heart was so full she thought for sure it would burst. It had taken a long time, a treasure hunt, and a heck of a lot of heartache, but finally she'd found the adventure and the treasure that would last a lifetime.

Dear Readers,

I hope you enjoyed the third book in this exciting and fun new collaborative series 7 Brides for 7 Brothers. I really enjoyed working with bestselling authors: Barbara Freethy, Ruth Cardello, Christie Ridgway, Lynn Raye Harris, Roxanne St. Claire and JoAnn Ross in bringing you seven incredible love stories!

If you are new to my books, I hope you will begin the journey with my Anderson Series, first book "The Billionaire Wins the Game." This is where a meddling father has a great time finding true love for his unwilling sons.

For more information on all my series and to sign up for my newsletter check out my website at www.melodyanne.com.

Do you want more Brannigan brothers? Knox's story is coming next from USA Today bestselling author Christie Ridgway. Here's the blurb ...

Knox

When super-wealthy father of seven Colin Brannigan dies and leaves each of his sons a bequest, Knox Brannigan believes he scored big and best with his legacy—a vintage Indian motorcycle. He's made a life out of rebelling against his father's focus on high-powered business and high-powered people, but this time Knox follows the old man's edict and takes it for a spin up the Pacific coast. When the machine breaks down he brings it to the shop listed in the owner's manual—the closest place in California that can find the right part and repair the bike. It means three days of loafing at a rundown surfside motel, but that means three nights of getting under the skin—and with hopes, the clothes—of the lovely but disapproving owner of the yoga studio next door.

Erin Cassidy practices yoga to discipline her heart, mind, and body. But all three go wild in the presence of confident, charming, and much-too-handsome Knox Brannigan. She knows his type. He claims to be a part-time bartender but Erin's sure that's code for fun, flings, and never settling down. After being burned before, she set strict guidelines about the men she lets into her life. Knox, with his sexy smiles and laid-back attitude breaks every one of them. It's only three days, she tells herself. If only they weren't followed by those three steamy nights…

Knox has always been a man who takes his pleasures where and when he can find them and to hell with the rules. Yet when it comes to his feelings for Erin, he discovers he's much more traditional than he ever imagined. It won't take deep breathing or mindful meditation but only being in her arms to turn the rebel into a lover.

38829285R00112

Made in the USA
Middletown, DE
28 December 2016